BLOOD FEUD

Higo, a Japanese railroad worker, kills two guards and escapes into Utah's canyonlands, and when Cal Mitchell goes after him — it's not just for the $500 reward . . . Along with his tempestuous passion for Modesty, dark secrets beckon Cal homeward, towards the mountains of Zion. He also seeks vengeance against the five Granger brothers. Blood flows and bullets fly as Cal steps back into his murky past. Can he find peace when the odds are stacked against him?

JOHN DYSON

BLOOD FEUD

Complete and Unabridged

LINFORD
Leicester

First published in Great Britain in 2010 by
Robert Hale Limited
London

First Linford Edition
published 2012
by arrangement with
Robert Hale Limited
London

British Library CIP Data

Dyson, John, *1937* –
   Blood feud.- -(Linford western library)
   1. Bounty hunters- -Fiction.
   2. Revenge- -Fiction.
   3. Western stories.
   4. Large type books.
   I. Title II. Series
   823.9′14–dc23

ISBN 978–1–4448–0949–7

Published by
F. A. Thorpe (Publishing)
Anstey, Leicestershire

Set by Words & Graphics Ltd.
Anstey, Leicestershire
Printed and bound in Great Britain by
T. J. International Ltd., Padstow, Cornwall

1

The great whaleback hill of Zion was darkly shadowed, its sheer wall of cliff rising a thousand feet high as beneath it in the distance a rider appeared miniscule as she rode her mustang up the incline.

The only watchers in this rocky wasteland would appear to be the little prairie dogs who stood on hind legs, pointed noses twitching before giving sharp barks and diving back down into their burrows. Or the ragged black ravens who swooped to caw harshly at this intruder to their realm. Human visitors were few and far between.

But up the mountainside a youth of sixteen years peered through a bronze pocket telescope and watched the girl straddling the horse with her bare legs, her homespun dress hoicked up around her thighs, her abundant black curls tossed by the incessant wind as she rode, bent forward, her hands gripping the reins as she urged the beast on.

Caleb Mitchell licked his lips hungrily as he registered the sway of her breasts beneath the dress. When she turned the horse into the dark slit of a narrow defile and disappeared from sight he closed the 'scope and slipped it back in his pocket. He gripped his rifle, turned from the cliff edge and headed back to the cave. It would take her a good fifteen minutes to climb the mustang up through the steep defile.

Above him on the mountainside were the sheep he had been sent to guard and on the wind was carried the tinkle of their bells and their pathetic bleats as they constantly sought nourishment from the scant foliage. It was a lonesome job and not one he much enjoyed, but after seven days he would be relieved by Aaron, who would take his turn for a week keeping at bay mountain lions, coyotes, eagles and other predators.

Cal scraped fingers through his long, blond hair, trying to tidy it, tugging it away from his eyes, and hitched at the crotch of his faded jeans for already he felt his body taughten at the sight of the girl. She had emerged from the gulch and dismounted, dragging the mustang by its reins up the last steep incline towards the cave.

'Hi,' Cal called. 'I been waiting for you.'

'Whoo!' Modesty exclaimed. 'Let me get my breath. It's quite a climb.'

Cal took her reins and hitched the horse alongside his grey on the platform of rock on a pinnacle of the mountainside. 'You got my dinner?' he asked, for want of anything else to say. He felt awkward and tongue-tied to see her again for her fresh-faced beauty and lucent eyes made his heart pound in his chest.

'What else you think I'm here for?' The wind plastered her dress tight against the slim curves of her body and she gave him a mischievous smile. She unhooked the pail of lamb stew from

3

the saddle. 'Shall we go inside?'

It was cool inside the cave out of the afternoon sun and the girl sighed with relief as she set the pail to one side and sank down, crosslegged, on a rough bed of pine needles covered with Cal's blanket. She tossed her wide-brimmed straw hat away. The two top buttons of her dress were already unbuttoned and she shook some air down her front. 'It's a scorcher out there. I'm all sticky.'

'Waal,' Cal grinned. 'We got our own shower out back.'

Modesty licked her lips, hesitantly. 'I didn't oughta. It ain't right. It's aginst God's law.'

She was older than him by six months and was well aware of the enormity of their sin. It could only end badly. But her heart was pounding with excitement like his, too.

'C'm on.' Cal was already barefoot and he knelt down to gently pull off her boots. 'Who gives a Goddamn?'

'Cal, don't blaspheme. What we're doin' is — '

He grabbed her hand and jerked her to her feet, leading her back into the recesses of the gloomy cave to where there was a natural grotto, a mossy pool into which they stepped, slipping into each other's arms, Cal hungrily seeking her soft, responsive lips, her body, as water dripped and trickled on to their heads through cracks in the great rock roof above.

Cal put down his hand to get hold of the damp of her dress and pull it up over her head. Modesty wriggled free and gave a groan of bliss to be naked and enwound with him in this foolish hot summer of their youth, rejoicing in the icy water on their bodies, in his touch. Clamped so tight, kissing, throbbing, thrusting, as if defying the world ever to tear them apart.

$\star$ $\star$ $\star$

It had started six weeks earlier on a day the patriarch, Gideon Mitchell had chastised his son, Cal, for some trivial offence and the youth had flared up, defiantly. Mitchell ruled his household with a religious fervour and had rough-handled Cal into the barn and set about him with his thick leather belt, his square-shaped black beard waggling furiously.

Cal had crawled up into the hayloft to escape his blows and it was there Modesty found him, comforting him with insistent words. The family were indoors at supper and she had brought him a few scraps of food, slipping out of the kitchen door in the dusk. The girl was as lithe and slender as a mountain cat but, Cal couldn't help notice, filling out in all the right places.

'I hate him,' he had hissed as he lay back in the straw. 'One of these days I'll be as strong as him and I'll fight him back, you'll see.'

'It's not his fault,' Modesty had whispered, caressing his shoulder and gently kissing his cheek. 'It's the Grangers who have soured him. Come on now. One must forgive.'

The Grangers were their nearest neighbours, with five lusty sons, who had grabbed the best land down on the rolling grassland valley of the Virgin River where they ran their cattle ranch. A latecomer, Gideon Mitchell had been forced to move on up to the rockier reaches of the valley which was only suitable for sheep or goats.

Mitchell had suffered insults and attacks from the Grangers. He could get no justice and his hatred simmered and burned like red coals.

'I ain't in a forgiving mood,' Cal had replied as he stared up into her dark, lustrous eyes as if seeing her for the first time.

Modesty had never touched him so intimately before. Leaning over him, she had smiled, mysteriously, stroked a finger down his cheek and murmured, 'C'm on, don't sulk.'

It was as if her touch had sent a jolt of electric current through his young body. A simmering fury still in him, he had grabbed her and twisted her down into the straw, kissing her with violent need, unheeding of her cries, 'No, Cal, no!' as he wrestled her into submission. Gradually her struggles against him had slowed. Perhaps she had not screamed because she did not want to get him into more trouble. She had lain, breathing hard, staring up at him, then raised her hands to draw his face close to hers.

★　★　★

'I've got to be getting back,' Modesty said now, coming from the cave to stare out at the maze of eroded forms, the spires and pinnacles and strange witch-like columns, thousands of them, that led on for fifty miles into the Badlands. 'It's a long ride.'

They had dried their clothes on the sun-hot rock and Cal tugged his spurred boots on his feet and crammed a worn Stetson down over his brow. 'I'll come with you part of the way.'

'There's no need, 'she said. 'What

about the stock?'

'They'll be OK till dark.' Cal fondled the nose of his four-year-old grey filly as he slipped the bridle in place. He and his brothers had brought in a wild herd they had trapped in a box canyon. He had broken and trained Smoke, himself, and loved her as only a youngster can love his or her first horse. He called to their old sheepdog, 'Patch, stay. Guard.'

The westering sun was setting alight the vivid oxide reds and yellows of the canyon walls while those in shadow mellowed into purples and blues as, on foot, he led Smoke down the rocky descent from the cave, followed by the girl. On safer ground he turned and gazed at her. 'Can you come again in a day or so?'

She met his steely-grey eyes and shook her head with a sad, sweet smile. 'Cal, this is wrong. I'm older than you. I never should have. I'm feared of God's punishment. No good can come of this.'

'I'm as old as you, near enough don't matter,' he protested. 'It's lonesome up here. I need you.'

'Cal, we must stop this. Don't you understand? You're my brother.'

He shrugged. 'Sometimes I don't feel like your brother. It's strange.'

He offered his cupped hands to give her a leg-up and she sprang lithely on to the mustang. 'Well you *are*,' she said. 'And I'm your sister. So let's go.'

★　★　★

A man in a low-crowned hat pulled down over his swarthy features to shield his eyes was kneeling on the rim of a cliff, his Creedmore rifle steadied on a rock as he fed a slug into the breech. 'There he is,' he muttered. 'And the purty gal. I'm in luck.'

He watched the two riders coming out of the mouth of the web of canyons and rock spires, known as the Maze for good reason, running into the harsh stretches of the Badlands. They were coming from the slit of a narrow ravine and heading at a fast lope across open ground. He couldn't miss.

Now! He squinted along his sights, squeezed the trigger . . .

Suddenly Cal saw the glint of sunlight on steel up ahead and, instinctively, jerked the grey to one side. Smoke screamed as the bullet ploughed into her. The filly's front legs buckled as she collapsed, blood fountaining from her chest, going down in a kicking paroxysm of pain. Cal kicked his feet free of the stirrups and rolled clear.

'Cal!' There was panic in the girl's voice as she heard the sound of the shot go bouncing off the great cliff walls. She wheeled the mustang back towards him. 'Are you all right?'

'Get down!' he shouted. 'Get in cover. There's some madman up there tryin' to kill us.'

Another rifle shot clapped out and, as he crawled towards his stricken horse, a slug tore through the sleeve of his homespun shirt. He reached the back of

11

the groaning, gasping grey and managed to jerk his rifle free of its scabbard. He levered the Winchester and sent a first bullet spinning towards the black puff of smoke on the rim of the hillside. In reply another shot cracked out and skimmed cutting and whining across the side of the grey, spraying Cal with blood.

The filly kicked and screamed again and, in a fury, Cal sent a fusillade of lead at the bushwhacker on the clifftop. He was about 400 yards off. Cal saw movement and fired the ninth and more from his magazine at a man in a dark suit and low-crowned hat who ran at a crouch out of the rocks, rifle in hand, scrambling away as Cal's bullets pursued him, and disappeared out of sight.

There was silence. Then they saw the attacker riding fast away along the clifftop. 'I figure he's had enough,' Cal called. He reached out and patted the warm hide, and his voice broke as he cried, 'Smoke's dead.'

'Why?' Modesty led her mustang

over to him and noticed the tears brimming in his eyes. She knew how close he and horse had been. 'Why should anyone do such a thing.'

'It wasn't Smoke he wanted dead: it was me.'

'But why?' she asked, her eyes troubled.

'Because they hate us.'

Modesty nodded, fearfully. She knew who he was referring to: the Grangers.

'It looked to me like that lawyer uncle of theirn, Isaac Granger. But I couldn't be sure.'

'What are we going to do? Maybe he's waiting on ahead. Cal, I'm scared.'

The youth reloaded the Winchester from his belt. 'If he is I'll be ready for him. Come on, we better get home. I'll come back for my saddle.' He looked sadly at the creature sprawled in the mud. 'Poor ol' Smoke. She was my best pal. Maybe I'll bring a shovel and bury her.'

Modesty could not help a faint smile at such a notion, but she squeezed his hand. 'Come on, Cal,' she urged. 'You ride the mustang.'

He nodded, caught the horse and jumped into the saddle, offering his hand to help Modesty clamber up behind. He spurred the mustang away at a canter. 'We better keep our eyes peeled from now on.'

2

'What was the girl doing up in the canyons?' Gideon Mitchell roared. 'And what were you doing, boy, leaving the sheep untended?'

'I was seeing Modesty safely home,' Cal shouted back. 'And it's a damn good job I was or she might never have got here. God only knows what that fella had in mind for her.'

'How dare you speak the Lord's name in vain? He sees everything, but that is not for you to judge.' The burly patriarch clawed at his black beard in exasperation. 'Haven't I taught you better? What's been going on? That's what I want to know.'

'It was Modesty's idea to take the boys some fresh food when they were up in the mountains. She volunteered for the ride,' his wife, Martha, butted in. 'How were we to know there was

15

some maniac prowling around up there?'

'Funny you never send any fresh food out to me when I'm wrangling mustangs or scything hay,' Jedediah Mitchell, the oldest son, bellowed. A younger version of his father, he was as broad, built like a barrel, with a bushy black beard, too.

'Why should we?' Martha snapped. 'You and Father get back to the ranch for supper.'

'You know who's behind it, don't you?' Jedediah replied. 'The Grangers. In my opinion whoever it was wasn't aiming to kill anyone. He was havin' some fun. He just killed the horse as a warning.'

'That's probably true,' the middle brother, Aaron, sneered. 'It's just Cal's imaginings.'

'I didn't imagine nuthin',' Cal fired back. 'He near took off my head a coupla times, like I've said. I ain't letting this pass. I'm gonna get whoever it was killed my horse.'

'You just wait until I've sorted this out.' Gideon was presiding over the breakfast table the next morning. 'I intend to visit the Grangers' ranch.'

'No!' Martha shrilled. 'That's what they want. You know we're outnumbered. They'll kill you all.'

Gideon knitted his brows, pondering this. 'Very well. Harness the wagon. We will all go into Temperance and demand a lawful investigation.'

He had been named after the Biblical leader in Judges who kept his land in peace for 40 years and fathered seventy-one sons. His own life did not match up. His first wife, Bathsheba, had given him two sons and had died of fever. He had taken Martha but, after producing Modesty and Cal, it seemed she was barren. She was a good woman but had become old before her time, scrawny and gaunt, her hair greying and thin, scraped back into a bun, worn out by work and worry, her face as eroded, it seemed, as the mountains all about them.

Gideon could have taken a third wife for he had come West in a wagon train of pilgrims, members of the Church of Jesus Christ of Latter Day Saints, who were escaping persecution for their practice of polygamy. Their founder, the prophet, Joseph Smith, he gladly followed. But Smith was dead. The new leader, Brigham Young, had founded Salt Lake City. His followers worked hard to make fruitful parched and unpopulated desolation.

One of the families, the Grangers, had taken a strong dislike to Young's autocratic rule and his hogging of the best-looking young women — he had twenty-six wives in his bedroom! They had broken with the church and moved far out, claiming the lush grassland of the lower valley of the Virgin River to run their cattle.

Gideon had decided to join them for he had come to the conclusion that Smith's laws were being perverted. He believed a man should have only two, or at the most, three wives. So with his young family he had followed the Grangers up into the Utah wilderness.

The Granger clan, however, were in no welcoming mood, and told Gideon to keep off their terrain and to move on higher up the valley. So Gideon had trudged onwards up towards the canyons. There the land was unsuitable for cattle with barely enough grass for a small, scrubby herd. He and his sons had raised their house, hacking at the unwelcoming ground to grow scant crops, and running sheep in the mountains. It was a hard life but they managed to survive with the Lord's help.

Today Gideon and his family, he, Martha and Modesty on the wagon, the three boys on mustangs, took a circuitous route through the canyons to avoid the Grangers' ranchland and eventually rolled into the small township of Temperance.

Adam, the father of the Granger family, had founded the township and welcomed tradespeople, so there was now a general store, the Zion Co-operative Mercantile Institution, a saddlery, blacksmith's, laundry, restaurant, flour mill powered by a water wheel, and a collection of dilapidated wooden cabins. Adam had insisted that all newcomers should follow his new religion, a cult he named The Brethren. He had built a temple for worship, but it had more in common with Baptists than Mormons.

When Adam died suddenly of a heart attack, his role as head of the community was taken up by his brother, a lawyer who had fought in the Civil War, Captain Isaac Granger. Needless to say he more or less ran the town. There was no saloon, gambling den or whorehouse, although often the Granger boys wished there were for attractive young females were as rare as hens' teeth in the vicinity.

When the Mitchell boys cantered in beside their father's wagon, lo and behold, there they were, the complete Granger brood, standing on the wooden sidewalk outside their uncle's law office as if the Mitchells had been expected: Joshua, Noah, Ephraim, Jacob and Paul.

Noah Granger was leaning against a post, one hand on the revolver slung on his hip. 'Waal, what do I smell?' he jeered. 'Them dang-bladded, shit-eatin' sheep-herders. They got their own stink ye can smell a mile away, ain't that so, boys!'

His brothers joined in the jeers and catcalls, apart from Joshua, the oldest one, a man as broad and hirsute as Gideon, and attired in a dark church suit. He raised his Quaker-type hat, nodding to Modesty. 'Quit it, brothers, they ain't doin' us no harm.'

'Let 'em try,' Jacob Granger growled, fingering a shotgun he held across his chest.

'Look at ol' Josh,' young Paul cackled. 'Like an old cat eyeing the cream. All he wants is to get into that hussy's calico drawers, if she's got any on.'

'Who wouldn't?' Ephraim Granger cawed, as the others laughed.

Gideon Mitchell's face was stern and wrathful as he drew the buggy in outside the law office. 'We've come here to make an official complaint. Where's the sheriff?'

'Old Cassius got kicked out,' Joshua replied. 'We got a new lawman elected by the town council last week.'

'Yeah?' Cal, on horseback, eyed the gang. 'We know who runs your poxy council.'

'Keep out of this, son,' Gideon shouted. 'I'll do any talking needs to be done.'

'It was my horse they damn well killed.'

Captain Isaac Granger had stepped out from his office. 'Who are you accusing, young man?'

'It was one of you. That's for sure. Tried to kill me, too.'

'Those are slanderous words,' Isaac put in, 'if you're suggesting one of us Grangers was involved.'

'Steady, Cal,' Gideon bellowed. 'I'll deal with this. I'll speak to the sheriff, if you don't mind, *Mister* Granger.'

He deliberately ignored the lawyer's military title now he was no longer a serving officer. It was only for show. 'Call him out here, or shall I go in?'

Like most of the ramshackle edifices on both sides of the dusty main street the lawyer's office was built of clapboard. Alongside was an adobe block, the sheriff's jailhouse, its windows barred.

The middle-aged Isaac Granger, neatly attired in a three-piece suit, cravat and polished boots, gave a faint smile of his thin lips and regarded them through the lens of wire-rimmed spectacles. 'I don't think you've met our new sheriff, Mr James Houck. It so happens we were buddies in the war.'

'Yeah,' the older boy, Jed Mitchell drawled. 'I bet you were.'

'Some of us were patriots,' the lawyer snapped back. 'Unlike you Mitchells. I didn't see any of you volunteer.'

'You can still see the yeller streak down their backs,' Noah hooted. 'Me an' Jake fought at Missionary Ridge.'

'The Rebs were already beaten and on the run by then,' Jed Mitchell shouted back. 'You ain't no heroes.'

'My boys were too young for that foolish conflagration,' Gideon put in, his cheeks flushing furiously at the insults. 'I had a holding to run.'

'Sound to me like a bunch of snivelling cowards.' A voice boomed out as a swarthy, thickset man stepped out of the jailhouse. 'Of course, that's just my opinion.'

Cal swung down from his mustang, his leather chaps swinging to the gait of one who spent much time in the saddle as he sprang forward and pointed a gloved finger into the stranger's face. 'You take that back or I'll make you choke on those words.'

James Houck had a curly mop of iron-grey hair. His thick moustache ran into a six-day stubble on his hefty, dimpled chin. He had wide, ape-like nostrils and his mahogany features split into a wide grin. By contrast, Cal's long

24

eyelashes, his chiselled high cheek-bones, gave him an almost feminine look, his ash-blond hair hanging over his brow and back over the knot of his bandanna. But his grey eyes were steely as he met the mud-brown ones of the new sheriff.

'You the kid who had his hoss shot?' Houck growled. 'You better come inside with any witnesses and give me the lowdown.'

His hooded eyes lazily lingered on Modesty as she stepped down from the wagon in her Sunday dress. 'Very nice! I can see why your assailant might have had plans for you.'

The girl eyed him, suspiciously. 'How did you know I was there?'

Houck shrugged his powerful shoulders in his tight blue, sweat-stained shirt. His short legs, with a .32 revolver hog-legged from a stout gunbelt, seemed too small for his body. 'I got informants,' he said.

Gideon jumped from the wagon and bustled forward. 'You seem to know a lot about things seeing as you've only been here a week.'

'You a witness?' Houck snarled. 'No, so keep your fat nose out of it. C'mon, honey, you first.' His strong fingers dug into her arm as he ushered her into his office. He turned to Cal. 'You wait outside.' He slammed the door in his face.

His office was sparsely furnished. Just a desk with a swivel chair, a big iron safe and a gun rack. 'You can have my seat, darlin'.' Houck thrust her into the chair, sat close to her on the edge of the desk, and gazed at her, lust smouldering in his eyes. 'Just give me the facts, sweetheart.'

In a faltering voice Modesty began to outline events. Why, she wondered, did this brute of a man make her heart beat so? 'The first bullet hit Smoke out of the blue — '

'You two rode outa the Slit?'

'The what?'

'The Slit. That's what they call it, don't they?' His lips curled back over strong teeth in a grin. 'That narrow gap in the cliff. The real question is what had you been doin' up there? Up to no good I'll be bound.'

'I didn't come in here to be insulted by you. I want my father to be here.'

'Insulted? What you talkin' about, sweetheart? He reached out and caught hold of a wooden crucifix hanging from a cord around her neck and drew her to him. 'You a good Christian gal, are you? The apple of your daddy's eye? And that brother of yourn? I bet he has fun up the Slit when you arrive.'

Modesty blushed deeply under her tan, trying to pull away from him. 'You've got a filthy mind. Let me go. I'm getting out of here.'

There was a hammering at the bolted door as Gideon shouted, 'What's going on in there?'

Houck grinned and dropped the crucifix back on to her breast. 'Maybe that fella who took a pot at you knew more about you than you imagine.' He went to open the door and she hurriedly squeezed past him and out into the sunshine. Houck stared aggressively at Cal. 'You, get in here.' He glanced at Gideon Mitchell and kicked the door shut in his face.

'Stand over there.' Houck sank into his chair, stuck his boots up on the desk, lit a cheroot, breathed out smoke and shook out the match. 'OK, what happened? Don't go tellin' me no lies, kid. I intend to get to the bottom of this.'

*   *   *

When Cal came out he found that his father had gone down to the wheelwright's to get the wagon fixed; Martha had bustled off to purchase coffee, sugar, sewing needles and so forth at the co-operative general store, while his brothers were humping out sacks of flour and splitcorn from the mill.

Modesty, in her white cotton Sunday dress, her hair in long plaits, looked as pretty as a picture as she stepped out from the ironmonger's, closely followed by Joshua Granger who was carrying a tin bath and some new buckets.

Jacob Granger was the only one of the five brothers who was married. His wife, Pamela, was gawky and shy, the daughter of the owners of the Vienna restaurant. To be generous, the giggly girl could only be described as plain. She had gone off with her husband to visit her parents and was probably stuffing pastries into her spotty face.

There was a dearth of fanciable females in the vicinity and the other brothers, like most sex-starved young men, strutted about looking for trouble. When they spotted Cal they skulked along the sidewalk to follow.

'I'll take those,' Cal said to Joshua. 'She don't need your help.'

But the burly Josh refused to hand over the bath and buckets. 'Get lost,' he squawked. 'You ain't needed.'

'It's you who ain't needed.' Cal caught hold of his shoulder and slammed a fist of jealous fury into his jaw. 'We don't need no help from you Grangers.'

Joshua stumbled back a trace, shook his head for a trice, like a puzzled dog, carefully placed the purchases on the sidewalk, removed his hat and black jacket, placing them aside. 'Excuse me, Modesty. This upstart young brother of yours needs educating.'

Cal backed away and slung a hard left, but Josh caught him in a bearhug, and headbutted him. Pinned in the powerful embrace, Cal jerked up his knee hard between Joshua's legs.

'Ouf!' Joshua groaned and flickered his eyelashes. Cal broke away and punched him in the belly. Josh roared like an outraged grizzly. Twice the weight of the youth, he leaped on him, crushing him like a ten-gallon wooden beer barrel, pinning him to the dust.

The yahooing Granger boys danced around them urging Josh to finish him. But hearing the commotion Jedediah and Aaron rushed up. The three Granger brothers engaged them with flying fists and kicking boots. The big bearded Jed could cope with two of them. But through the dust swirl Cal could see Aaron getting the worst of it, knocked to the ground and being severely beaten.

'Goddamn,' he groaned, unable to move.

'Duh!' Joshua's eyes almost crossed as Modesty swung a log picked from a pile on the sidewalk and cracked him across the back of his thick skull. He passed out cold and she helped roll him off Cal.

'He was only being helpful,' she said. 'What gets into you?'

'I dunno.' Cal ran to help Jed and Aaron who were under attack from Ephraim, Noah and Paul.

The crash of a revolver brought the pugilists and onlookers to attention. 'Hold it,' James Houck shouted. 'That's enough of this. I've a good mind to toss y'all in the hoosegow.'

Modesty filled one of her buckets from a horse trough and tossed it over

Joshua, who spluttered and sat up, shaking his head. 'Sorry, Josh,' she said. 'Hope I didn't hurt you.'

'No, that's OK, Modesty,' he replied. 'A pleasure to meet you.'

Cal was helping the bleeding Aaron to his feet. 'Let that be a lesson to 'em,' he said.

'You!' Houck was pointing a finger at him. 'You're the troublemaker here. I'm gonna be watching you.'

Cal picked up his Stetson and dusted himself down. 'Yeah, I'm gonna be watching you, too,' he called back. 'In fact, you look a lot like that killer on the cliff. One day Smoke is gonna be revenged.'

'Come on.' Modesty tugged at his arm. 'Ain't you done enough harm? Ma an' Pa are waiting and they don't look none too pleased.'

3

Cal's earliest memory was of a cabin being set on fire, of screams, gunshots, horses whinnying, men's boots stomping the floorboards, bodies sprawled dead, blood — so much vivid red blood — pooling across the floor, a woman's arms reaching out to take him, hug him to her, escaping through the maelstrom, lifting him into a light buggy and racing away through the moonlit canyons.

The charred remains of that cabin still stood far out on a lonesome hillside above the river and since coming across it he had sometimes returned, drawn back by an unseen force, trying to remember who were the ones killed in the cabin that night and who the killers. It was as if the mountain wind brought voices calling to him. But they were only ghosts . . .

And now it was happening again. A

week after the fist fight in town Cal was woken in his bed by men's shouts, the flicker of tar torches, the thud of hoofs as horses careered about the yard. The barn was ablaze and against its glow darkly silhouetted were masked riders, one hurling a blazing brand towards the house. He heard Martha's scream of panic, Gideon's roar of anger. Jedediah and Aaron rolled from their bunks and for moments stood petrified, listening, horror in their eyes. 'Get your guns,' Jed cried. 'We're under attack.'

Although a religious man Gideon Mitchell had bought the boys rifles and insisted they learn how to use them from an early age. They weren't just for shooting at wolves and coyotes, or foxes that raided the chicken coop, but for a time such as this.

Cal grabbed his Winchester and leaned from the open window cracking out a shot at two riders who went cantering by. One wheeled his whinnying mustang, a carbine gripped one-handed under his arm. Cal saw the flash of gunpowder as the man returned fire. The bullet smashed into the woodwork of the window and from the light of the flames he saw that his assailant was wearing a flour sack mask, open slashes revealing only the eyes and mouth. Whoever it was spurred his horse prancing away to the other side of the house before Cal could get another bead on him.

He dodged out into the kitchen parlour and saw Modesty in her nightdress staring at him. 'What can I do?' she pleaded.

'Get a box of spare ammo,' he yelled. 'We gotta stop them getting the horses. Stay inside. I'll be back.'

Aaron had taken up a position at a back window and was firing out at the attackers. 'There's about seven or eight of them,' he cried.

'Yeah. Cover me. I'm going out.' He agilely leapt from the window and landed on the balls of his bare feet in the dust. There was the crash of a shotgun and he saw his father, his square black beard jutting out over his nightshirt, standing at the house corner. He let loose a second barrel of shot. A raider veered his mustang away narrowly avoiding the volleys.

'Stay here, boy,' Gideon roared, as Jed started after the masked man, his rifle raised. 'And you Cal, keep in cover.'

But what Cal feared was happening. Not only was the barn ablaze but the gunmen had knocked down the pole gate of the corral and were hallooing and firing off shots to send the horses skittering free.

'You bastards!' The burly Jedediah, in his long johns, ran out in the night towards them and Cal raced after him, levering another slug into the Winchester's breech. He fired to no effect as he ran, then saw a rider, his mackinaw billowing, his eyes burning in the slits of a mask, charge his dun at Jed. The big revolver in his fist blazed and Jedediah went rolling like a potted rabbit to lie still.

The rider cocked his strange 'hand cannon' and charged on towards Cal who ran to meet him. He was intent on getting an accurate aim when his bare toe hit an abandoned branding iron in the grass and, in agony, he toppled off balance as the murderer blasted a bullet over his head.

Cal groaned, nursing his toe, as the raiding party joined forces and galloped away into the night.

His father Gideon lumbered after them, loosed another barrel of leadshot at their backs, and slumped to his knees over his eldest son. He raised him in his burly arms and began to sob when he realized what Cal already knew. 'Why us, Lord?' he wailed, as Martha joined him. 'Why have you abandoned us?'

Cal was hopping around, his stubbed toe fiery. 'I gotta try an' catch one of the hosses,' he cried as Modesty arrived, thrusting a box of a dozen .44s into his hand, her face dismayed. 'They're going after the sheep. They're headed up the canyon.'

'You can't do anything, Cal,' she screamed. 'They'll kill you, too.'

Aaron seemed to be in a panic, hurling water from a bucket at the burning wall of the barn, then trying to catch the chickens that came running out, only succeeding in making them rush back into the inferno.

Standing in his pair of frayed jeans, Cal hesitated, grabbed a rope hackamore from the corral rail, then reloaded from the box of bullets and raced away searching for the horses. Maybe they wouldn't stray more than a mile or so. After half a mile, his bare feet cut by the rocks, he began to wish he had gone back for his boots. But in the moonlight he saw one of their mustangs calmly chewing at a thistle. Cal crept up, caught him by his mane, slipped the hackamore over his nose and leapt on to him bareback.

It was no easy job guiding the mustang but he got him going at a fast lope along Four Apostles canyon, riding beneath the shadows of the four mysterious mountains until he saw the great whaleback cliff rearing up ahead.

'Oh, no. Jeesis Christ! They're going to.'

He hauled the mustang in and stared up at the rim of the cliff at the silhouettes of seven riders scurrying back and forth against the night sky. He could hear them firing off their pistols and whooping as they rounded up the Mitchells' flock of sheep. And, relentlessly, they were driving the scurrying, bleating, grey mass towards the edge of the cliff. Cal watched the sheep tumble one after another off the sheer 500-foot cliff, careering to their deaths on the rocks below.

Cal raised his rifle and took careful aim, squeezing the trigger to send lead spinning. But it was a long shot. The distant raiders on top of the ridge turned to look in his direction, then made off over the side of the mountain. Which route they took through the maze of intertwining canyons would be anybody's guess.

The youth kneed the mustang forward, almost reluctantly, until he reached the great pile of bloody sheep at the foot of the cliffs. He felt sick in his stomach as he went close up to them on foot. There were a few still giving agonized cries, but most were in contorted positions, their eyes glazed by death. Cal used up all his bullets putting the half-alive ones out of their misery. Then he limped back to the mustang, patted its neck, and headed home.

★   ★   ★

All that remained of the barn were smouldering struts and a pile of ashes. Gone was their summer hay so laboriously scythed from their one good field only weeks before. Most of the chickens had been too panicked to escape and lay dead with their feet sticking up in the air. The Mitchells had no well, fetching their water from the river a quarter-mile off on a daily basis.

'I tried to save the barn,' Aaron wailed, 'but once the rain barrels were empty . . . '

They all stood in the darkness for a long time staring at the flickering flames. The loss of Jedediah was too immense to come to terms with yet. He had been such a larger than life character, the image of his father, but jollier, full of energy, the first to get stuck in with his pitchfork if any job needed to be done.

Gideon had brought out his knife and dug a big bullet from his son's chest. He studied it in the lamp-light. 'You know anyone who packs a pistol uses a slug the size of this?'

'It's one of them big, snub-nose manstoppers,' Cal said. 'I've heard about 'em. But never seen one. They churn about in the body doing terrible damage.'

'At least,' Martha said, 'he died instantly. He didn't suffer for long.'

'We find who uses a bullet like this we got our man.' Cal took the slug from

41

his father to examine it. 'Can I keep this?'

'Oh, yeah,' Aaron scoffed. 'I suppose you're gonna track him down.'

Cal shrugged. 'You never know. I guess I was lucky I tripped on that dang running iron or he'd have got me, too.'

'Huh, you allus have to try to make out you're the hero,' Aaron sneered.

There was no love lost between the two brothers. They had squabbled and fought since childhood. From the first Aaron had seemed to resent Cal's arrival, always siding with his big brother, or sucking up to his father, agreeing with everything laid down as family law.

As a teenager Cal had grown increasingly rebellious, arguing with Gideon, skipping his chores and paying the price. He even dared to criticize their religion. The house reverberated to Gideon's religious mania. He was forever thumping his fist on the table, demanding they recite the scriptures. If Cal refused, he knew it was at the risk of a whipping. In fact, he sometimes felt like a cuckoo who had been dumped in this strange nest.

But, as they helped Gideon pick up Jedediah, carry him into the house and lay him on the kitchen table, he sensed that this was only the beginning of their grief. Cal watched as candles were lit both ends of the table and his family knelt praying through the night for his soul. It seemed like they were all cursed.

Towards dawn Gideon rose from his knees, his Bible in his hands. 'The Lord in His wisdom chose to take our fine boy,' he intoned. 'We — '

'Wisdom?' Cal blurted out. 'You call that wisdom? Where's the wisdom in making us break our backs over this rocky old bit of ground and giving the Grangers all that green grass? If He's so wise, why'd He take a good man we need? Why'd He trip me up just when I'd got a bead on that killer?'

'Cal,' Martha moaned. 'Not now.'

'You dare to insult your brother's

memory.' Gideon seemed almost dumb-struck. 'You — '

'It ain't Jed I'm insulting, it's you. We know who did it. Why don't we ride now? Go an' get 'em.'

'No,' Martha shrieked. 'There's seven of them, with Houck and that hired man. You've no chance.'

'Go to your room, Cal,' Gideon ordered. 'I understand your rage, but your mother is right. We must show caution. Tomorrow we will take Jedediah's body into Temperance and demand justice.'

'Justice?' Cal scoffed, as he left them. 'Houck's their hired gun. A fat lot of justice you'll get from him.'

He went outside. Bitter, acrid smoke from the fire still hung around the house. He tossed the manstopper in his palm. 'It was him, all right. I recognized his eyes.'

Suddenly he felt Modesty's arm slipped into his. 'Cal, don't go upsetting Father. Not now. He's had a terrible shock. He and Jed were very close. I

44

fear he's a broken man.'

'Ach! All this prayin' gives me the creeps. We can't let 'em ride roughshod over us. We gotta fight.'

'I see.' From behind them came Aaron's mocking voice. 'Comforting the unbeliever, are we? I see whose side Sister's on.'

★ ★ ★

Gideon Mitchell dressed his dead son in his church suit and tie, laid him in the back of the wagon, and with Martha and Modesty beside him, the two boys on their mustangs as outriders, he headed for Temperance again. 'He's going to get a good funeral,' he said, 'so all can see just what's going on.'

Uncaring about being accused of trespassing, he drove across the Grangers' open range and was surprised to see that on its edges several sections had been taken over by sodbusters. 'So the Grangers ain't drove you off with their guns?' he called out, as he halted besides a man busy building a frame house. 'Like they did t'others.'

'Nope.' The man paused, hammer in hand. 'They sold us this. Mind you, it ain't freehold. Isaac Granger drew up some sorta lease, full of legal mumbo-jumbo a man cain't understand.'

'Means he ain't letting go of the reins,' Gideon muttered and nudged the wagon horse on. 'Means he can tell 'em how to vote.'

When they trailed into Temperance a small crowd gathered to watch in silence as they carried Jedediah into the funeral parlour. The big-bearded patriarch turned to them and shouted, his voice almost breaking, 'They murdered my boy, set my house alight, and killed all our sheep. They wore masks, but we know who they were and I guess you do, too. Are you gonna stand for this?'

The crowd stood, almost shame-faced, making no reply, except for one man, probably one of the new home-steaders, who called out, 'What do you expect! You let them filthy beasts get on our grass, that's what you get.'

'Who are *you?*' Cal spat out. 'Granger's stooge? Did he bring you in here specially to say your bit?'

An angry murmur ran through the crowd. There was no getting away from the fact that sheepherders were hated throughout the West. Especially by cowmen. This was no isolated incident. Over in Wyoming hundreds of thousands of sheep had been slaughtered and herders shot down in such attacks.

When they came from the funeral parlour, Gideon Mitchell, his shotgun under his arm, led his family over to the jailhouse. It was no surprise to find James Houck standing outside glowering at them beneath the brim of his flat-crowned Stetson.

'Yeah, whadda ya want?' he growled, malevolently.

'I want to know who murdered my son last night and I want — no, I *intend* — to see him hanged.'

'Yeah,' Cal put in. 'He was riding a

big dun much like that one hitched outside your jail. Come to think of it, his build was much like yourn, big chest and shoulders and skinny li'l legs.'

'You accusin' me?' Houck growled, his hand moving to cover the butt of the .32 pig-stringed to his thigh.

'Keep out of this, Cal.' Gideon Mitchell put out a hand to restrain his angry son. He didn't want a double burial on his hands. 'The fact is you, I mean the gunmen, were all masked. The bullet that killed my son didn't come from a small calibre revolver like yours.'

'Who's to say he ain't got another damn gun hidden away some place?' Cal yelled.

Isaac Granger had been watching and listening from the window of his office. With a faint smile on his face he stepped outside on to sidewalk. 'Did I hear you Mitchells accusing our law officer of murder? That's ridiculous. He dined with me out at the ranch last night and we were up until four o'clock discussing business and playing poker. The boys can swear to that.'

'I bet they can,' Cal drawled.

'You better watch it, dim brain.' James Houck took a half-smoked cigar from his mouth and tossed it at Cal, who stepped out of its way and levered the Winchester as he did so.

'Yeah, come on. Try me.'

The crowd moved out of danger as Gideon again put up an arm to hold Cal back. 'Don't, Cal. He's trying to provoke you.'

'Would I?' Houck's hand was on the grip of his .32. 'It's him doing the provoking.'

'Threatening a law officer,' Isaac Granger tuttutted. 'That's an indictable offence.'

'Maybe I'll do more than threat,' Cal gritted out.

'Look, you've not a shred of evidence that Mr Houck or any of my family were involved in this attack,' Granger said. 'Maybe they were that gang of *bandidos* who've been hiding out in the Badlands.'

'Ridiculous!' Gideon cried. 'What *bandidos*? Why should they do that? What would they gain?'

'For God's sake, Mitchell, don't you realize that everybody hates sheep-herders? Isn't this area barren enough without sheep ruining the grass with their close-cropping and sharp hoofs, turning everything to dust?'

There was a murmur of agreement from the crowd and Houck joined in, 'Yeah, and stinking up the land and the waterholes. That upsets cattle and horses. Everybody knows that. They didn't oughta be allowed.'

'There's no proof of that,' Gideon bellowed. 'That's just a myth. We ain't done no harm.'

Houck gave his wide-nostrilled grin. 'Seems to me like you ain't got no proof of nuthin', Mitchell. Ain't it obvious you ain't wanted around here? When you gonna get that through your thick head? It's time you were moving on.'

Gideon stared back at him, then at the lawyer. 'You ain't running us out.

You might own these folk and this town but you don't own me. We're going to give our son a Christian burial in this town's graveyard. Then we're going back to our ranch. You — you've corrupted our religion with your guns and greed.'

With great dignity he turned, ushering his wife and daughter through the crowd. 'Come along, boys. We can do no more.'

But Cal broke away, raising his rifle and calling out, 'You've asked for it, Houck. You killed my brother. I know that.'

He aimed the rifle and tried to squeeze the trigger, but Houck's revolver came out fast as a prayer and its bullet cut searing through the side of his chest. It was like a lightning bolt had hit him. His rifle went flying as he was hurtled back to sprawl in the dust.

Modesty screamed and ran to kneel over him, cupping his head in her arm. 'Cal,' she sobbed, as she pulled off his bandanna and tried to staunch the blood. 'Somebody, please, help.'

'Aw, ain't that a touching sight?' Houck, holstered his smoking .32, removed his hat and ran fingers through his curly mop and down to thoughtfully stroke his thick moustache.

'I oughta arrest him. He could get two years for attacking a lawman. But I'm the kind-hearted sort. Take him and go.'

They carried Cal over into the shade as someone ran to fetch the doctor. Granger beckoned Houck into his office. 'Why didn't you kill him?'

'Because I like playing cat an' mouse,' Houck leered. 'An' because you ain't paid me yet.'

'What do you mean? I gave you five hundred.'

'Yeah, well, I'm greedy. I need five hundred more if you want the job done.'

'Listen, James, I've got you this easy little number. The town council pays you fifty dollars a week and you ain't got much to do,' the attorney said. 'Don't push me.'

'Maybe I should tell folks about how you an' me ran that prison camp, starved, beat and robbed them Rebs blind.' Houck smiled like a cat over cream. 'Maybe they'll figure the noble Captain Granger weren't such a wonderful war hero.'

'OK,' the lawyer spat out. 'You get another five hundred when he's dead.'

4

Cal woke from a tumult of dreams of flames and pursuit by masked men to find himself in a tangle of bedclothes on his cot in his familiar timber-walled room. Outside, the sun was shining and the few remaining chickens were quietly clucking. A fly was buzzing about the room. Cal listened to the sounds and felt a great sense of peace and relief to be still alive.

'So, you've decided to rejoin us?' Modesty called. She heard him groan as he inspected his bandaged wound.

'How long I been under?'

'Two days. I guess the bumpy wagon ride home was too much for you. You passed out and have been in a coma. Doc figures you should be OK. How do you feel?'

'OK.' He met her sloe-dark eyes. 'Better for seein' you.'

'Good.' She sat on the edge of the bed and gently stroked his sweat-damp hair away from his eyes. 'Seems like you're a lucky sonuvagun. His bullet hit your ribs which deflected it off your lungs. It passed right through. If it was a clean wound you should pull through, being young and healthy and with me to nurse you.'

She gave her impish, cheek-dimpling smile, tossed back her mass of black curls and sprang lithely to her feet. 'Can you sit up?' She helped him to do so, arranging his pillow. 'Do you fancy some chicken broth? Looks like we'll be eating chickens for days.'

'Sure.' He leaned back on the pillow. 'I'm starving.'

Later, after she had spooned some of the hot broth down him, washed him and changed his dressing, he murmured, 'If you're gonna be my nurse I think I'll lie here for good.'

'Huh, I don't think so. I aim to get you back on your feet. I've got to go. There's so much to do.' She picked up his tray, turned at the doorway to smile at him. 'Try to get some more sleep.'

There was little rest for a female on a smallholding like this. Cooking, washing, weaving, sewing, mending, sweeping, chopping firewood was just a start. On top of this, Modesty had to drive the horse and wagon to the river to refill their buckets and tubs. She had gutted and plucked so many chickens in the past two days she was sick of the stink of their insides. Those that wouldn't keep had to be buried. Then there was the herd of goats to be milked and cheeses to be made. Modesty and her mother kept the dairy equipment in a cool cave up on the hill. At least she didn't have a child to attend to. Looking after Cal had taken up a lot of her time.

'Oh, yeah, it's OK for some, ain't it?' Aaron scoffed, when he and his father returned to the ranch at sundown. 'Got outa all the dirty work, ain't you?'

Gideon had decided to save as many of the fleeces as possible to sell on. It had been a hellish job the past two days hacking the coats from the bloody, fly-buzzing creatures, treading through slime and guts, the bloody corpses piled up at the foot of the cliff, attended by hopping, feasting crows and ravens, blinded by sweat in furnace heat, watched by furtive coyotes and by eagles spiralling above.

'We ain't gonna be able to eat much of the mutton, but I'm gonna have a good try before the maggots get it, so get the oven going, Mother.' Gideon had come stomping into the kitchen, plonking down some bloody meat. 'We've put what else we saved up in the dairy cave. It's the coolest place.'

Aaron had washed himself in the river and was towelling his black curly hair. He had similar dark-eyed looks as his sister but not her sunny nature.

'How's the bullet hole?' he asked. 'Does it hurt? Serves you right for trying to play the hero. That man Houck's fast. You didn't have a snowball in hell's chance.'

Cal shrugged. 'I know that now. I'll

have to learn to be faster than him.'

'Aw, grow up. Talk some sense. You always were a damn fool.'

Aaron went back into the kitchen for supper, slamming the door. Cal grimaced at the pain in his shoulder and sighed. 'I ain't gonna git much sympathy from him.'

★ ★ ★

Cal knew he was lucky to be alive. Most men who suffered gunshot wounds, if not cut down immediately, generally suffered a lingering death from blood poisoning when bits of metal and powder in the wound set off infection. Within a fortnight he was back on his feet and fit enough to busy himself about the ranch.

Gideon had employed a Paiute Indian to tend what few sheep and lambs had escaped the attack on the mountainside so there was no need for Cal to be out there now. Or for Modesty to visit him.

One morning he climbed up to the cave on the mountainside and found the girl, in her summer cotton blouse and skirt, sitting spread-legged on a wooden stool, her cheek pressed to the side of a goat as she kneaded its udders. He listened to the rattle of the milk hitting the pail and watched as her own breasts stirred beneath her blouse.

Cal stole in behind her, squatted down and slid his hands about her to fondle them firmly. 'Guess I must be feelin' like my old self again,' he whispered.

Modesty tensed. 'Don't! You nearly made me jump out of my skin.'

'I need you,' he pressed, kissing her ear. 'It's been an age.'

'Well, you better go an' feel your ol' self, not me.' She struggled to her feet, swinging the bucket out of the goat's way. 'Leave me alone. Mother, anybody, could come in.'

'I don't care.'

'But I do. Just keep your distance from me in future.' She backed out of the cave door. 'You've caused enough trouble lately. I don't want any more.'

'You know you want to,' he pursued. 'It's terrible being so close to you all the time and not being able to.'

'You're gonna have to get used to it, Cal, because I'm not doin' anything any more, not around here. Aaron's already got his suspicions. He's jealous of you, you know that. I'm scared.'

'What of?' he jeered. 'God's judgement?'

'Who knows? I'm sorry, Cal, that's how it's got to be. Please, if you love me, leave me alone.'

But that would be easier said than done. For Cal, perhaps for both of them, their love or lust for each other had become like a raging fire.

★ ★ ★

James Houck cantered his big dun along a ridge of hills leading down to the Mitchells' ranch. It was a fine summer morning, a scent of juniper on the breeze. He paused in a clump of pines and studied the spread. He could hear the sound of hammering as the three Mitchell males rebuilt their barn. Suddenly he caught sight of the girl riding a mustang away from the ranch following a trail towards the river. 'Waal, whadda ya know?' he muttered, stroking his heavy moustache, as she passed beneath him.

It looked like she had a bundle of washing tied behind the saddle. She was riding astride, her skirt hoicked high to reveal her shapely bare legs. He licked his lips and tugged his hat down over his brow. 'Looks like my lucky day.'

There was a series of cascading small falls where the water poured over the rocks forming pools. Modesty had jumped down beside one and emptied the bag of clothes into it. She took a bar of carbolic soap and began busily scrubbing away. James Houck hitched his dun to a pine branch and climbed down to her carefully. He grinned as he crept up, the sound of his boots drowned by the noise of the falls. Modesty started with surprise as she felt his hands grip her waist. 'Oh, no,' she groaned, thinking for a second it was Cal. 'Not again!'

'Whadda ya mean?' Houck growled in her ear.

'Who else has been pawin' ya?'

The girl gasped with fright as she spun around and met him face on. Houck's brown eyes glowed with mischief as he twisted her down on to the flat rock she had been kneeling on. 'No need to tell me, I can guess. How's that brother of yourn? You oughta be grateful I didn't kill him.'

'Let me go.' She pummelled his powerful chest with her fists, writhing and wriggling to escape, but he held her wrists in an iron grip and gave a deep-chested, mocking laugh.

'Steady,' he said. 'I don't wanna hurt you. We can do this the easy way, or the tough way. It's up to you, sweetheart.'

'I ain't your sweetheart, you loathsome man.' She twisted her head away as he pulled her to him and tried to kiss her lips. 'You stink. You disgust me.'

Houck's spittle trickled down her cheek as he slavered over her, gripping one hand in her thick curls to hold her still. 'Who you tryin' to make out you are? Some li'l, never-been-kissed virgin gal? Go on, struggle, you wildcat. I know all about you.'

Modesty squeezed her lips firm as he managed to press his mouth on hers, tempted to bite him, but her heart was pounding with fear. Houck had a dark coldness, an evil strength, as if he could do anything. And she was well aware what he wanted to do.

To avoid his anger, his fists, she decided it might be best to submit. It looked inevitable. This man could easily kill her. So she went limp in his arms. 'Take it easy,' she said. 'You're hurting me.'

'Ha!' He gave a guttural cry of triumph. 'I thought you'd see sense. You know what the robbers and *bandidos* call me where I come from? The

Avenger. Nobody bothers me. They know it ain't wise.'

'Where do you come from?' she asked. 'You're a bit of a mystery.'

'Yeah? Is that what attracts you? I knew you fancied me when you saw me in my jailhouse. You protested too much. Ain't that so?'

'There's *something* about you.'

He had cast his Stetson to one side and sweat trickled from his greying curls as he leaned close over her. Modesty tried not to recoil as his lips slurped on hers. He had her pinned to the rocks, his hands in her hair. She began to run her hands up and down his strong back. He had forced his legs between hers and she felt helpless.

'Something bestial about you.'

'Yeah, that's what you like, eh, gal?' he grunted.

'It's not comfortable here. Couldn't we lie down in the shade?'

'Nah. This suits me. I ain't gonna take long.'

Modesty let him kiss her again, this

time responding to his hunger with her tongue, urging him on. Her fingers reached down and found his weapon. The .32 was holstered on his left thigh. She gripped the butt with her right hand, slipped it out and thudded the barrel with all her strength against his temple. She went on pounding him with the heavy butt end until he slumped into unconsciousness. She heaved him away from her and gasped with disgust. She flung the revolver as far away as she could into the fast flowing river and went scrambling, slipping and sliding over the rocks, leaping on to her mustang and kicking it into action, riding away as fast as she could.

★ ★ ★

'It's Houck. He tried to rape me,' Modesty sobbed out, as Martha caught her in her arms. 'I'm afeared he's dead.'

'What?' Gideon Mitchell roared, when he was given the news. 'Aaron, saddle the horses. Get the guns. We will go settle accounts with Houck. If you haven't killed him, Daughter, I will.'

But there was no sign of the Temperance sheriff when they arrived at the scene. The washing was still in the pool but the place was deserted. 'Look at this,' Aaron shouted, pointing to spots of blood on the rock. 'Something's been going on.'

'Well, he's certainly not dead, more's a pity.' Gideon tugged at his beard in agitation. 'Will the man give us no peace? We will have to go into Temperance and see just what he has to say. No doubt he will deny ever having been here.'

'Are you sure he *was*, sir?' Aaron suggested slyly. 'Do you think Modesty is telling the truth? Haven't you noticed? She has been acting very strangely lately.'

'You think so? She has always been a devout, truthful girl.' Gideon pondered the situation. 'Seems like just one thing on top of another. Will we never have any rest?'

66

* * *

Gideon was torn between riding into Temperance the next day, or killing two birds with one stone, so to speak, finishing the drying and combing of the sheepskins and packing them on the wagon so that full use could be made of the long journey into town. Martha said that she wanted to take goat cheeses and a pile of chicken pies into market to sell, so, as she busied herself getting them ready, the trip was postponed for several days.

'What's the matter with you?' Cal demanded. 'He attacked Modesty. He ought to be in jail. Are you all scared of him?'

'We all need to cool down. Not go in there in a red-hot rage,' Gideon thundered. 'And, Cal, you won't be coming. That's an order. I don't want a repeat of last time.'

When the morning came for them to depart, Gideon climbed on to the loaded wagon beside Martha, with

Aaron mounted on his horse, rifle in hand. 'Cal, get on with the barn roof. I'll be wanting to see what you've done when we get back.'

He had decided that Modesty should not have to face Houck so she and Cal stood there as the wagon rolled out. When they were out of sight the youth tentatively touched her, putting an arm about her waist.

'Oh, Cal!' She swung into him, burying her face in his chest. 'Hold on to me. I'm so frightened of what might happen. It's as if we're all trapped in Houck's web.'

'I won't let him get you,' Cal, replied, stoutly. 'I'll be ready for him next time.'

'I had better get on with my chores,' she said, breaking away from him and returning to the kitchen. 'And so had you. You don't want to get Father mad.'

'Aw, they'll be gone all day,' he coaxed. 'It's a long drive.'

She had picked up some wooden bowls from the table and was taking them to wash when he caught hold of her. 'We're alone. Don't you see? We can do what we like.'

'No, Cal.' But Modesty didn't sound too sure as she let him hold her and run fingers through her hair. 'I must say, it is nice to get rid of them for a while.'

'Yeah, all them religious ravings, all that quoting of Bible texts. The Old Man seems to have got even more demented and bitter since Jedediah was murdered.'

'Can you blame him?' she murmured. 'That's nice.'

He had raised her chin with his finger and was gently stroking her cheek. 'Hey, why not go an' lie down on their bed? Let's make the springs groan like they do.'

'No, I couldn't.' Modesty tried to hold back. But her eyes, too, were full of devilment. 'Not in there.'

'Why not?' Cal scooped her up, carried her into their parents' room, and laid her on the big bed. 'Let's pretend we just got wed.'

Modesty's heart was racing. She

knew it was a terrible sin. But, as he kicked off his boots and jeans she began to unbutton her blouse, awed by his slim sculpted body. There was no way she could resist. He rolled on to the bed to caress and soothe her, removing her clothes until they were both naked. But they didn't waste much time on preliminaries.

Suddenly it was as if their bodies were on fire and it was a race against time . . .

They lay out of breath, tangled in each other, afterwards, and Cal laughed, joyously. 'That was the best.'

'Yes,' Modesty murmured. 'It gets better every time.'

Suddenly they heard the whicker of horses, the creak of wagon wheels in the dust of the yard, Martha's voice calling out, 'Cal, Modesty, where are you?' She was already in the kitchen. 'The mare's gone lame. We're back.'

'Oh, no!' Modesty hissed. An awful dread seemed to freeze the moments of time. There was nothing she could do but spring to her feet in panic, try to wind the sheet around her, leaving Cal naked, calling out, 'I'm in here. Don't come in!'

'What are you doing?' Martha was standing in the bedroom doorway. Behind her came her husband's heavy tread. 'My Holy God!' he shouted. 'What Satan's work is this?'

'What do you think we're doing?' Cal replied, sullenly, as he sat on the bed edge, pulled on his crumpled jeans. 'I'll give ya three guesses.'

His father's belt was whistling through the air, the buckle end hitting him across the face. Cal raised an arm to fend off the rain of blows from the enraged man. He vaulted back over the bed and picked up his Winchester from the floor, always kept close in case of Granger attacks.

'You damn well hold it right there, you fat fiend,' he shouted. 'That's the last time you ever hit me.' Blood was trickling from his cheek as he jerked a slug into the breech. His eyes were fixed on his father. 'Get outa my way. I'm leaving. You won't never see me no more.'

His mother screamed. 'No, Cal. Don't do this.'

'Yes, go,' his father thundered. 'Get out of my house. This is a God-fearing household. You filthy, lousy, snake in in the grass. How could you do this to us?'

'I didn't do it to you: I did it to her,' Cal muttered, as he gingerly moved around the bed, keeping them covered. But later he thought perhaps he did do it almost to spite them.

'My beautiful daughter, my innocent,' Gideon sobbed, the belt still raised in his fist. 'How could you abuse her, you devil's spawn? I should have known.'

'Yes, she is beautiful and innocent,' Cal agreed, beckoning to them with the rifle to get out of his way. 'Too damn beautiful to live with you.'

'What?' Gideon made to swing the belt at him again, but Cal skipped past him, backing out of the door. 'I'm warning you. I'll use this if you do that again. I mean it — '

Suddenly he turned and saw Aaron with his own rifle raised, a scowl of jealous hatred on his face. 'You always were the troublemaker,' his brother screamed, and pulled the trigger. Instinct made Cal squeeze his own trigger, hardly realizing what he was doing. Aaron's bullet creased his cheek, thudding into the wall. Cal's hit his brother full in the chest, bowling him backwards to lie prone, an agonized look on his face as blood began to pump from his shirt front.

'Oh, Lord have mercy on us,' his mother screamed, running to kneel over their dying son.

Cal's rifle was wrenched from his hands by Gideon, who growled at him, 'You will pay for this. I am taking you into Temperance to be hanged.'

Cal leaned back against the wall, too shocked to resist. He shook his head. 'He shouldn't have . . . ' Then nodded and muttered, 'Yeah, I guess you must.'

5

James Houck stood at the doorway of the jail, his head bandaged, but a wide grin on his ugly mug, thwacking a piece of rubber hose into the palm of his gloved hand. 'Welcome to your new abode. I'm gonna enjoy interrogatin' you the way we did in the army.'

'I'm here voluntarily,' Cal said as he warily stepped down from his mustang. 'I don't want no trouble.'

'No,' Houck leered, 'I bet you don't. Killed your own brother, did you? Now ain't that a how-de-do?'

'That's enough, James,' Isaac Granger cautioned. 'He's made a complete confession. He don't need no softening up.'

Gideon Mitchell, who had brought his dead son, Aaron, into town in the back of the wagon, accompanied by Martha and Modesty, had decided that as Granger was the only lawyer in town,

and also the county prosecutor,
Cal up to him.

It was bitter cordial for Gi⟨
swallow, to have to consult with
enemy, but what else could he
was still in a state of shock.

The lawyer was caught by s
too. 'You've got the right to send
circuit judge but that would
wait of several weeks. Or you ca
before the town judge tomorr⟨
get it over with.'

Thoroughly crushed, Gideor
that the town judge, an Irish
lion, Eamonn McIntyre, was a
drinker who had his own still
woods at the back of his house,
was one of Granger's stooges a⟨
would get little mercy from him

'What do you want, Cal?'

'Hell, let's get it over with.'

'Right.' The lawyer had his cler
down Cal's statement and that
father. 'You'll be arraigned to ap⟨
court with relevant witnesses ton
at nine o'clock. You'll be k⟨

stody. Have you any guns with you?'

'My rifle's in the saddle boot.'

As Cal was being handed over to the
eriff, three of the Granger brothers
me cantering into town and reined in
a swirl of dust. Grins spread over
ah, Eph and Jake's faces as they
wped at what was going on.

'There's one more thing.' Gideon pointed
forefinger at Houck. 'This thug of a
-called sheriff of yours attempted to
e my daughter the other day. I want
m charged with that.'

Again Captain Granger looked mildly
rprised. 'What you got to say to that,
mes?'

'I'd say she's a lying bitch.' Houck
uched his head. 'Look what she did to
e. It's me who oughta be charging her
ith assault.'

'Explain just what happened, Sheriff,'
e lawyer said. 'For the benefit of this
traged father here.'

'What happened?' Houck growled,
nacking the lead-loaded pipe in his
lm again. 'Sure, I was out by their

place riding along the river when I stopped to pass the time of day with the gal. Guess what? She started making eyes, flirting with me, making suggestive remarks, showing off her thighs.'

'That's a lie!' Cal yelled.

'Let the sheriff say his piece,' the lawyer advised.

'Waal, as we all know young Modesty Mitchell's a real pretty piece. Immodesty might be a better name. Before I barely knew what was going on she was canoodling and close-up kissin' me. Talk about hot. What would any red-blooded male do but respond?'

'Whoo!' Ephraim, still on horseback and craning to hear, gave a whistle. 'You lucky dog!'

'Lucky? That two-timin' li'l cockteaser suddenly snatched out my pistol and cracked me over my temple. Kept on hittin' me until the blood flowed an' I passed out. When I come to she was gone.'

'These are heinous lies!' Gideon roared. 'My daughter would never behave like that. The fact is this man tried to rape her and she had to hit him to escape.'

Houck poked at his wide hairy nostrils and grinned. 'First I figured it must be somethang I said. Then I realized the hussy's got a grudge aginst me and had planned the attack all the while. She near broke my skull.'

By now a number of rubber-neckers had gathered round to wonder at his words. 'The sheriff's talkin' about the Mitchell gal,' a woman hissed. 'I always thought she was a shady one. There's something amiss with that family.'

'So, Mr Mitchell?' The lawyer gave a sarcastic smile. 'Do you want your dear daughter to have her reputation tarnished in court? Personally, I don't think you'd win.'

'Forget it,' Gideon muttered. 'Take your prisoner, Houck. But you treat him right.'

'Who me?' Houck reached out to grip Cal's arm. 'Hey, boys. Can you give me a hand? This guy's a dangerous character. I'm gonna have to manacle him, wrists and ankles. I might need some help.'

'Sure thang, Sheriff.' Jake jumped with alacrity from his horse, followed by his brothers. Shouting and laughing they helped Houck push Cal into the jailhouse. 'This,' Jake beamed, 'is gonna be a pleasure.'

★ ★ ★

'How do you plead?' the judge asked.

'I killed him,' Cal said, 'an act I will regret to my dying day.'

'That may not be so far away.' The prosecutor, Isaac Granger, smartly attired, as usual, gave a wry smile. 'Your honour, we needn't beat about the bush. The prisoner admits he shot down his own brother, Aaron Mitchell. I demand the ultimate penalty.'

There was a loud murmur of assent in the crowded courthouse. 'Hang him!' a woman screeched.

Old Judge McIntyre banged his

gavel. 'Order!' he shouted, mopping his brow. 'We'll have less of that.'

Dr Henry Dixon rose to his feet. 'Your honour, I have offered to represent the prisoner. Although he admits shooting the deceased, he did so in a moment of surprise and acting in self-defence. Therefore he pleads not guilty to the charge of homicide.'

'Oh, he does, does he? Is that so, young man?'

Cal had been brought into court still chained by his wrists to his ankles. He shrugged. 'I guess.'

The judge stroked his six remaining hairs into place across his bald pate and frowned, uncomfortably, at Dixon. 'So what qualifications have you, might I ask, Doc, to represent him?'

Dr Dixon, in suit and starched collar, his hair slicked back, spoke in rapid staccato voice. 'I studied law at my college back East before switching to medicine. I believe that entitles me. I am concerned that he will not get a fair trial at the hands of the prosecutor.'

When Granger rose to protest, the doctor raised his voice and spoke over him. 'I am also concerned at the way the Mitchell family has been persecuted in this community, and the way the prisoner has been treated in custody. When I gained access to him this morning to look at a gunshot wound received at the hands of the sheriff, which I have been tending recently, I found numerous bruises on his body, evidence of a severe beating.'

'Is that true, Mitchell?' Judge McIntyre demanded. 'Were you beaten up in jail?'

Cal shrugged again, his chains rattling. 'Sure, I guess they give me a seein' to, but they didn't have it all their own way.'

'We had to restrain him,' Houck growled. 'In my opinion he's a dangerous criminal. He's already tried to kill me and made wild accusations against the Granger family. The kid's crazy. A mad dog. If we don't put him down he'll kill again.'

'To be sure I don't like the sound of

81

this,' the judge remarked. 'I'll be having a short adjournment to consult my law books.'

He shuffled off out to a back room to fortify himself with stiff slugs from his bottle of moonshine. 'Very well,' he slurred, when he returned. 'Let's hear the wishnesses.'

So, one by one, Cal's mother, father and sister were ushered in and forced to swear on the Bible to the truth of their words.

The bearded patriarch's voice boomed out, 'Cal and I had an argument, the nature of which I do not intend to go into. I was forced to chastise him. I began to larrup him with my belt. At that he snatched up his rifle, said he was leaving and threatened to kill me if I tried to stop him.'

The prosector interrupted. 'Surely the court should be told what this argument was about.'

Gideon glowered at him, sternly. 'That is our business, not yourn. Nor anybody else's. Personal family business. Suffice to say his behaviour could not be tolerated in my house.'

'Do you believe Cal would have carried out his threat?' Dixon asked. 'Or was it a bluff? Would he have killed you?'

'Of that I am not sure.' Gideon pondered a while. 'He certainly cocked the hammer ready for use, but that might have been just show. He has always been a wild boy, often at loggerheads with Aaron, when he was alive, and with me. In the heat of the moment, perhaps . . . no, in all truthfulness I do not think he would. Not me.'

Captain Granger jumped up again. 'But you say he had enmity towards Aaron? Isn't it true that in his wildness he turned the rifle on his brother? He intended to and did kill him.'

Gideon shook his head, mournfully. 'How can I tell? All I know is that he turned to leave the room, his rifle still raised. From the kitchen outside I heard two almost simultaneous shots. I found Aaron dying in a pool of blood.'

When the prosecutor probed further, Gideon slapped his hands to his ears and roared, 'It is God's judgement upon me and my family. Why He should cast us out I do not know. It is a terrible torment to lose two sons and maybe a third now.'

His wife, Martha, grim-faced in black fustian, gave similar evidence. 'Cal allus was the wild one, causing trouble,' she said. 'Yes, I believe he deliberately shot Aaron down.'

Modesty, too, was in black mourning apart from her straw sunhat. She appeared tense and grief stricken and did not meet Cal's eye as she spoke. 'Cal killed Aaron. Who fired first? I do not know,' she murmured. 'Did he intend to kill Aaron when he fired? Yes, I believe he did.'

'There, you see!' The prosecutor sprang up, raising a finger to the judge. 'Did you hear that, your honour? She says Cal intended to kill Aaron.'

The judge hiccupped and mopped

his florid face again. 'Well, you generally do intend to kill 'em if you shoot at someone, don't you?'

'Quite. Now, if this argument was of such violent nature what provoked it, girl? Surely the court is entitled to know?'

'To be sure. Come on, my dear,' the judge coaxed. 'You tell us.'

Her eyes downcast, Modesty lied, 'I have no idea. It just flared up out of nothing.'

Cal was similarly evasive over that question. 'I dunno,' he drawled. 'Can't recall. We was allus arguing over somethang. When he hit me with his belt I jest got mad.'

'And you deliberately shot and killed your brother,' Captain Granger shouted.

'Not exactly. Aaron fired a split second before me. Outa the blue he came at me with his rifle, so I replied.'

'There was no malice aforethought in this case,' the doctor stated, in his closing speech. 'A clear case of self-defence. The charge should be dropped. To impose the death penalty would be absurd. This has been a most unfortunate tragedy. Hasn't this family suffered enough?'

The jury was a cross-section of male voters who had arrived in the small town founded by the Grangers: blacksmith, miller, storekeepers and suchlike.

'Right, you'd better be off to debate this,' the judge told them, and hurriedly returned to his own room and his bottle of hooch. It did not take the jurors long and they trooped back in to announce, 'Not guilty.'

Maybe they had had enough of being pushed around by the Grangers. Maybe they agreed with the doctor. There were shouts of both anger and sympathy among the noisy crowd at the decision.

Houck's face looked thunderous as he was forced to unchain Cal and return his rifle. 'Don't worry,' he snarled, 'you ain't gonna get away with this.'

Cal met his regard, pursed his lips,

but did not reply. What use were words? He swung around, rifle in hand, and headed for the livery where Gideon had lodged his stallion.

The Mitchell brothers had trapped the feisty wild beast and his harem of mares in a box canyon in the mountains and brought them in. First Jed, then Aaron had claimed the horse in terms of seniority, but now it was rightfully his. The big stallion kicked and pranced and was still difficult to get a saddle on, but that was the way Cal liked it. Plenty of fire 'tween his legs. He leaped aboard, slipped boot toes into the bentwood stirrups and, holding Nero back, went high-stepping up the main drag.

The Granger brothers, all five of them, had been in the courthouse and now were lined up outside the jail watching him. Noah was leaning against the wall idly, but ominously, swinging a hangman's noose from one hand. The lawyer and Houck were standing in the shade of the sidewalk outside Granger's office staring at him.

Doctor Dixon, on his more quietly behaved mount, clipped along up the street beside Cal. 'Well, you're a free man. What are you going to do now?'

'I didn't ask for your help, Doc. I was prepared to take the consequences. Anyway, thanks. How much do I owe you?'

'Nothing. It's *pro bono*. Volunteered my services for the good of the community.'

'Yeah, well, I figure this community would have been glad to see me swing. To tell you the truth I don't know what I'll do now. Maybe stay. Maybe move on.'

Cal had spotted Gideon, Martha and Modesty coming out of the funeral office and taking their seats on the wagon. He slowed Nero. Dixon called out, 'Whatever you do, good luck,' and rode on.

'Yeah, maybe I'll need it,' Cal muttered, as he drew the stallion in beside the wagon.

'If you've come to beg forgiveness you're wasting your time,' Martha cried. 'The burial's tomorrow but you'd better stay well away.'

'You ain't welcome at the ranch, boy,' Gideon said, gruffly. 'All we want is you outa our sights.'

'What about you, Modesty?' Cal asked, in a lowered tone. 'I'm going away. I'm asking you, come with me.'

Modesty glanced at him, her eyes, beneath the straw sombrero, dark and intense. 'I don't ever want to see you again, Cal. I hate you. It appals me, what you done. Don't you ever try to touch me.'

He had reached out his gloved hand to her, but she brushed it away. 'Leave the girl alone,' her mother hissed. 'Can't you see you've done enough damage?'

'You have brought the Lord's calumny upon us,' Gideon roared. 'One day you'll burn in the pit.' And he angrily whipped the wagon's pair away.

Cal watched them go rattling out of

town. He assumed they would return for the burial in the morning. He tugged his hat down over his eyes, wheeled the stallion around, glanced at the watching Grangers, and gave the horse his head to go galloping out of town. He would bypass the ranch and head into the Badlands.

★ ★ ★

He felt more like an outlaw than a man who had just been set free as he eased the stallion into a steady lope and passed beneath Perdition Mountain. 'I hate you.' Her words burned into him, spurring him on. 'Don't you ever touch me again,' she had whispered. 'You appal me.'

He allowed the horse a brief drink, filling his own wooden canteen, when they reached a shallow stream, a mountain tributary of the higher reaches of the Virgin River. Its red and green lower valleys had been left far behind by now. He went splashing on his way along the rocky bed of Canyon of the Spirits, its sheer walls towering over him to provide cool shade. It was familiar territory for he had often wandered here as a boy, and it was true that one seemed to hear the whispering voices of the dead, though what they said he could never discern.

When he came out onto open ground he saw the great, crimson-walled rincon of rock rising a thousand feet high and rode on under it until he reached the Slit, the narrow gully that led through and up to their cave. He paused for a few minutes, sitting in the saddle, remembering the summer idyll. Then he spurred the horse on. It was all in the past now.

He pulled the stallion to a halt again when he reached the burned-out cabin that had once been his home, peering into the charred timbers. As always, voices there seemed to speak to him, but again they were voices in the head of a child who had yet to learn to speak, mystifying but telling him *something*.

Just what, maybe he would never know.

It was then that he suddenly saw the line of riders silently following and his mouth went dry at the thought of the hempen rope around his neck. Not four, but seven horsemen of the Apocalypse, it seemed to him, darkly silhouetted against the lowering sun as they rode up the hillside towards him.

He jerked the Winchester out of the boot and took aim from the saddle at the leading rider. 'They ain't gonna get me so easy,' he vowed, but, as he squeezed the trigger, the stallion pranced impatiently and the shot whistled over their heads.

'Hagh!' Cal yelled, spurring Nero away as the men surged forward. They were about half a mile off. He had to get higher, reach the rim, get out of their range. The powerful, deep-chested stallion gave him the advantage, eating up the ground with ease. Cal knew that on the other side of the ridge the vast amphitheatre of the Badlands began. If he could reach its maze of ravines he might have a chance of escape.

He heard the crack of a rifle report and he instinctively ducked his head into the stallion's flying mane as a bullet whined and ricochetted off the rocks. Panic gripped him as a fusillade of shots rent the air, their reverberations booming off the cliff wall and rolling away. Lead zoomed past his head.

'Go, Nero, for God's sake.' he yelled.

The big horse pounded and scrambled up the last stretch. It was only a hundred or so yards now, but Cal gritted his teeth well aware that any second an accurate shot could send them tumbling. It was a race for life against death. Another volley of shots sent bullets ripping past him. But he reached the crest, looked back and saw the Grangers — for the Grangers it must be — surging up after him again.

He could hear their angry shouts and raised his rifle to give them a victorious wave of foolish bravado. It was not over yet. What to do? Cal's mind flashed between finding cover, attempting to pick them off, or making himself scarce as fast as he could.

Before him stretched the jumble of exotically eroded rocks. An army of witchlike columns, with high-pointed hats, stretched away towards the setting sun which painted them in yellow and crimson. This was the point where Cal had always turned back, these seemingly unending, intertwined ravines that went on for as far as the eye could see.

'A hell of a place to git lost,' he muttered, but the Grangers were getting nearer. It was his only option and he sent the stallion ploughing down from the rim through a scree of sand and rubble until he reached firm ground of a narrow ravine's floor.

Where it went to he had no idea, but the Grangers, and probably Houck, had reached the crest and their bullets were spurting into the dust about him. Cal cruelly spurred the stallion and sent him galloping full stretch along the canyon. He turned in the saddle and saw his pursuers heading along the rim as if they thought they could cut him off.

'Oh, no!' he groaned, as the ravine seemed to curve back towards them. Yes, there they were, careering down from the rim towards him. 'Jeeeis Christ!'

Cal could see the canyon looping into another bend so he put the reins in his teeth, raised the Winchester as he rode, quickly relevering the trigger guard to eject cases, and cock the weapon simultaneously, to send lead flying towards them. At last, success! One of the men and his horse somersaulted into the dust.

But it was a desperate, grim race as he grabbed the reins again, jabbed the rifle back into its boot, and standing in the bentwood stirrups, hanging low over Nero's head sent him galloping towards the shade of the next canyon bend.

Again he made it unscathed before his pursuers reached the firm ground. The mouth of another ravine yawned before him and he lunged the galloping horse into it praying that it wouldn't be a dead end. From then on he played a cat and mouse game, dashing from one canyon to the next, pulling the stallion in, and listening, heart thumping, for sounds of pursuit. At first there were voices, men's curses, the drumming of hoofs and twice he hid with the horse in clumps of eroded rocks and watched them go rattling by.

But gradually the sounds grew faint and he breathed more easily, bending forward to stroke the stallion's sweat-streaming neck. 'I figure we're safe, boy.' It was already growing dark and he had lost all sense of direction. 'We better find someplace to sleep and head on in the morning. God knows what you're gonna drink.'

★ ★ ★

'He'll be lucky if he gets outa that hell's maze alive,' James Houck growled, as his party retraced their steps along the canyon to the foot of the rim where Ephraim Granger's horse was sprawled, its eyes glazed, dead.

'Did you get him?' Eph asked.

'He got away,' the lawyer, Isaac, replied. 'But he'll be back one day. I can bide my time.'

'Just what the hell you got aginst that boy, anyhow?' Houck asked. 'You seem almighty fired up to get him.'

'I'm a man of the feud,' the prosecutor said. 'I don't forget. This is a dark secret in my life, one of hatred, one of blood.'

'Aw, come on,' Joshua called. 'He's gone now so let him go. We got to be heading back. You can ride up behind me, Eph.'

In fact, Josh was thinking of Aaron Mitchell's funeral the next day. He had no wish to miss it. He planned to offer Modesty his sympathy. 'I'm pretty sure she's got a soft spot for me,' he told Ephraim as they jogged along. 'In a way I'm glad we didn't kill her last

97

remaining brother. It wouldn't have done my chances a lot of good.'

'What in tarnation you talking about, Josh?' Ephraim protested. 'A Granger cain't get involved with a Mitchell.'

'If I wed her she'll be a Granger.'

'*Wed* her?'

'Yes. I intend to offer her my hand.' The brawny, bearded Joshua gave a chuckle. 'In fact, that ain't the only part of my anatomy I intend to offer her.'

6

'We just got to keep following the sun,' Cal said, as he let the stallion lap water poured into his Stetson. But already half of the once full canteen was gone. He took a mouthful of the precious liquid himself, but even before the cork was back in place his lips were dry. 'We'll find a way outa here, boy.'

A mustang was renowned for being able to travel long distances with little food, but Nero was a big horse and needed sustenance. He sure wasn't finding much nibbling among the rocks at the thorns. You wouldn't find many, or any, wild bunches venturing into this maze of ravines. In fact, few humans dallied there either, except, maybe, some crazy old prospector seeking the magic lode, *bandidos* on the lam, or a wandering war party of Paiutes.

The latter thought brought a chill to

his spine even in this 120° heat on Gabriel Fahrenheit's scale. It was now high noon, the sun directly overhead so a man was more likely to lose all sense of direction. The airless gullies were as hot as a bakehouse. Cal slashed with his knife at a juniper branch, fashioning its fork into a pick to stab into the cliffside and climb to the top. His shirt was clinging to him and sweat trickling into his eyes. At least there was a welcoming breeze on the crest but what he saw did not hearten him. Just a great empty expanse of eroded ridges going on and on and the deadening silence of the desert.

He scrambled back down to Nero. 'Let's go. I think we're headed the right way. Least, I hope we are.'

It was a frustrating business, twisting and turning, sometimes having to retrace their steps or climb over a crumbling barrier of shale to find some way through. Occasionally he would slash at a cactus, try to suck liquid from its interior, which could be painful, to say the least. He had left in such a mad hurry he had brought no food or supplies. There was no sign of game in this wilderness. But the stallion suddenly shied as a rattlesnake reared up. It had been sunning itself on a hot rock. Now it was clattering a warning, fangs ready to strike. Instinctively both rider and horse leapt aside. Cal pulled the Winchester from the boot and circled around it. The rifle's long barrel made it awkward to handle at close quarters, but his second shot blew its head off.

'At least I got supper,' he murmured, as he picked up the squirming beast.

He managed to find enough bits of dry wood to make a fire that night but, as Cal chewed on the rattler and peered at the eerie shapes of the rocks in the flickering light of the flames, he had never felt so sad, lonesome and alone. An outcast, torn away from his one true love.

'I got to put it all behind me,' he muttered as he lay back on his saddle, gripping his Winchester. 'If that's what she wants, an' if we ever git outa here, I'll start a new life. Forget her. Become someone new, someone else.'

He watched a pale globe of moon rise in a starry sky and vowed, 'One day I'll go back and face Houck.'

* * *

He rose about 3 a.m. and made an early start, the blueish moonlight casting its glow across the crags. He wanted to be like the nocturnal animals, get as far as he could then rest up in the shade through the hottest part of the day. The stallion was a strong beast but the lack of water was telling on him. His eyes had gone dull, his nostrils dry and he would suddenly stagger off course or flounder in the sand. Cal walked him for a few miles to conserve his energy, then rode again when his boots gave him hell. On and on they trudged, seeming to get nowhere. His spirits soared when he spotted a waterhole, but dipped when he tasted its brackish contents. It was alkali, undrinkable. When the sun reached its zenith its fiery rays bounced off the rocks into his eyes making his head spin. He began to get the staggers himself, his lips parched and cracked, as he pushed on through the gullies and ravines. The only signs of life were turkey vultures circling on the thermals up above, watching and waiting . . .

When he slumped down in the shade of a cliff and eased off his boots Cal wondered if he or the horse would get out of this barren furnace alive. A terrible exhaustion took hold of him and he lay back and sank into the grip of deep sleep.

The crash of thunder woke him like the clash of a thousand drums and cymbals tearing the heavens apart. Great black clouds rolled in from the east and he felt the blessing of blobs of raindrops on his face. A sliver of lightning shivered through the air, its fork daggering earthwards. 'Christ!' he cried, jumping to his feet as another blob of lightning seemed to explode in his eyes.

He hurriedly unbuckled his belt and tossed it with his spurred boots and Winchester well away, then removed the bit and bridle from the whinnying, terrified horse, and his saddle too, hanging on to Nero with a lariat around his neck. In a sudden calm he managed to quieten him, slipping the end of the rope tight about his forelegs to hobble him.

Another almighty crash rent the low-hanging clouds. Cal gave a whoop of joy and tore off his clothes until he was naked, laying them on the rocks to wash. As the full force of the storm hit them he danced around glorying in the sheets of rainwater in his hair and on his body, excited by fizzing lightning bolts. 'Yah! Missed me!' he yelled.

Just as suddenly the storm had passed and was blown away to leave clear skies and sunshine again. But, as the hobbled stallion hopped to drink at a small stream fed by spouting gullies

Cal hurried to fill his canteen and even his hat with the life-saving cool water.

'Hey, maybe ol' Gideon was right!' Cal laughed merrily at the idea, although somehow doubting it. 'There *is* a God up there looking down on us.' He waved to the departing clouds. 'Thanks, Lord, anyway.'

Both man and horse went on refreshed and with gladdened hearts and in the afternoon of the next day found their way out of the maze, climbing up to a ridge to see a valley with a river running through it, bordered by clumps of cottonwoods and greenery. Even more surprising they could see not far away square-shaped adobe buildings of a village or town.

'Whoo!' Cal looked back at the fifty-mile stretch of eroded ravines that had taken them three days to cross. He had only a few dollars in his pocket but it would be enough for a pail of split-corn for the stallion and a meal of some sort for him. 'Nero, ol' pal,' he cried. 'We've made it.' And he nudged him with his knees down towards the town.

★　★　★

Caliente, meaning hot, was a good name for this town, but it was also an oasis of cool. There was just a sprinkle of houses, the 'dobes of the Mexicans, which had been there for a century, intermingled with a few of timber boards erected by white settlers. A peaceful place, right out in the middle of nowhere.

There was a general store selling saddles to safety pins, a livery, bakery, blacksmith's and not a lot more. Cal was lured through the bead curtain doorway of a *cantina*. The thick adobe walls kept it shady and cool. There were a few Latinos and Anglos sitting around drinking and smoking. They eyed him curiously. The Mexican behind the bar beamed at him. '*Buenas tardes, señor?* Wha' you wan', hey?'

106

'You got a glass of cold water?' Cal drank it down in one swig. 'Can I have another? I got a helluva thirst.'

Ham and eggs, tinned tomatoes and tortillas had never tasted so good. Cal savoured every succulent mouthful. A pink blancmange to follow made him feel like he'd found paradise. He washed it down with mugs of thick black coffee.

'I don't have much money,' he told the proprietor when it came time to pay. 'You any idea if I can get any work around here?'

'You do some dishes?' The Mex pointed to the kitchen. 'That'll cover it.'

Over the next few days he found Cal a variety of small-paying tasks with other residents, splitting logs, painting a barn, helping plough and sow a field with corn, striding from one end to the other, back and forth all day into dusk, broadcasting seed by hand from a pile held in an apron.

But soon the jobs ran out. He was sitting in Pablo's *cantina* wondering what to do, where to go, when a gnarled old rancher swung from his horse outside and strode in. He gathered from his conversation with Pablo, as he sat at the bar supping a tomato juice and beer, that the old guy ran cattle on a spread out in the hills.

'I'm looking for a place as a cowpuncher, 'Cal said, introducing himself. 'I can ride and shoot: — '

'Sorry, son, I've been having to lay men off. Business ain't good these days. There's been a run on the banks. Have a drink?'

'I don't drink. I mean alcohol. My old man didn't approve. Come from a town called Temperance, which speaks for itself.'

'Aw, that mealy-mouthed crowd. You the boy who came through the Badlands? That's quite a feat. Not many men get through, or even attempt it.'

'I don't blame 'em,' Cal replied. 'I'll try and find another way round if I ever go back.'

'Aw, go on,' the rancher urged. 'One

of these won't hurt you. We call 'em red beers. Pablo, two reds, *por favor*.'

Cal took a tentative swig. 'Yeah, thanks. It tastes real nice. If my ol' man could see me now!'

The rancher grinned. 'This ain't exactly Sodom and Gomorrah. Talking of which, why don't you go try your luck in Goldfield. That's one wide-open town. You might make your fortune.'

'How's that?'

'Ain't you heard? They've struck a rich vein of ore. Folks are flocking there. If I was any younger I'd be heading there, myself.'

'How do I get there?'

The old guy pointed a finger out of the door. 'Head north-east through the gap in the hills, across Frenchman's Flat, past the Timber Mountains and on across Sarcobatus Flat. A two-hundred-mile ride mainly across dry scrub but if you made it through The Maze you can get there easy enough.'

'Through the gap . . . ? Could you give me them directions again?'

'Sure, pal, I'll draw you a map.' He produced a notebook, tore out a page and licked a pencil stub. 'You got the Pahranagat Range on your right side. That's where I got my spread. And the Sheep Range on the left.'

'I guess you'll be at each other's throats. They were where I come from.'

'No, that's all a myth. Sheep don't do no harm to cattle. I run both. In fact, there's more profit in sheep. Have another beer.'

'Nah, I'll get you one, mister.'

'OK. So you more or less keep going straight as the crow flies. You'll need to take a coupla canteens of water. There ain't much anywhere this time of year.'

'Yeah. Thanks.' Cal tucked the map in his shirt pocket. 'I'm gonna be more prepared this time. You say there's gold for the taking?'

'Sure, so I hear.' The rancher grinned. 'Just buy yourself a pick and shovel. You can't go wrong.'

★　★　★

In some ways he was sorry to leave the verdant Meadow Valley Wash, as it was called. The folks in Caliente had been real friendlly. They didn't object to him sleeping under the colonnade of the sidewalk, making a corner of it his spot where he could leave his rifle, his horse and what few belongings he had while he did his odd jobs. Nobody would have dreamed of stealing them. What a marked difference to his past life when, on their trips into Temperance, his family had been treated with scorn and cold hostility. Cal had come to believe that was the norm.

The old rancher had been right about one thing: once past the Sheep Range there was little sign of water. Frenchman's Flat proved to be just that, mile upon mile of arid desert scrub disappearing into a heat-haze. But Nero had an invigorated spring in his stride and at 7,000 feet altitude the high plateau was cooled, at least, by a breeze. Cal had come outfitted with three big canteens of water, beef jerky to chew on, flour, and a small sack of splitcorn for the stallion. There was also a trail to follow, the chapparal trampled down by a herd of beeves headed for Goldfield, no doubt to feed the hungry miners. Little wonder that this area all the way down to the Mexican border was marked on maps as The Great American Desert. There were numerous tales of emigrants in wagons losing their way and dying of thirst and starvation, apart from Indian attacks. 'We just got to keep on goin' until we get there,' he gritted out, as Nero ate up the miles.

His spirits soared as, on the fourth day, rounding a pyramidal clump of bare rock he saw a jumble of timber houses with, on their environs, the smoking chimneys of smelting works and the wheel shafts of mines. Goldfield!

7

The wide, dusty main street between the stores and houses was quiet at this time of day because most of the male population was busy labouring many hundreds of feet underground in the mines. But to Cal the array of two — and three-storey shingle-roofed houses on both sides, the proliferation of advertising signs above the sidewalks, the buggies, wagons and horses patiently waiting by the hitching rails, and the variety of goods on offer made him feel that he'd been living on the moon.

Apart from saloons, beer parlours, a meat market, billiards hall and general merchandise emporium, smaller, more exotic businesses clamoured for space along the sidewalk. There was Chiatovich and Co's 'Fresh Fish and Oyster Bar', though where they caught them Cal hadn't a clue. Smith's Secondhand

Furniture had, of all things, an upright piano amid its jumble of tables and chairs. Fancy cakes and pastries were displayed in Flourmegon's Buffet window, from which drifted an appetizing scent of coffee. There was a jewellers with a plate of solid gold false teeth offered at a bargain rate. And The Manhattan, a haberdashery and dress shop, dummies displaying 'the latest New York fashions'.

'Maybe I better git myself some place to sleep tonight,' Cal drawled to Nero as he let him drink at a water trough and hitched him to a rail, 'before I take in the town.'

There was a big sign stuck out high on a wall above. Hotel Esmeralda. A young lady, obviously a fan of The Manhattan fashions was decked out in an emerald-green dress of taffeta cut low across her bosom. Her flour paste face was wreathed by auburn ringlets. She was taking the air outside the hotel door, which was jammed between two stores. 'This way, cowboy,' she fluted, giving him a ravishing smile of painted lips, as if he was expected. 'Straight up the stairs. You'll have a wonderful time at The Esmeralda.'

'I will?' His spurs clattered as he climbed to a landing where a dark, Spanish-looking lady, with a heavy moustache, more soberly dressed, greeted him at a reception desk. 'Yes, young sir? What's your fancy?'

'You got a nice soft bed?'

'We certainly have. Clean and lice-free. Sheets changed twice a week. This is a luxury establishment.'

'Good. I'll take it for the night. How much will that be?'

'The whole night? You got that much stamina? Most of our guests pay for an hour.'

'Nah, an hour ain't long enough. I've been sleeping among rocks and rattlers. I need some shut-eye.'

'Maybe you misunderstand the nature of our business, young man. Most gentlemen don't come here for shut-eye, as you call it.'

'What *do* they come here for?'

Madame Moustache, as she was locally known, raised her eyes with exasperation. 'Genteel conversation and relaxation.'

'Genteel conversation . . . ?' Cal glanced beyond her into a parlour where he could see a girl in red silk stockings, blue pantalettes, a gauzy robe and little else, lounging on a *chaise-longue*. 'Relaxation . . . ?'

'Yes. However, if all you want for starters is to sleep I dare say we can accommodate you. That will be two hundred dollars.'

'Two hundred?'

'I thought that might make you change your mind. If you'd just like an hour in bed that will be twenty.'

'Twenty!'

'Yes, as I said this is a high-class establishment. All our girls came straight from a nunnery.' The madam's demeanour suddenly hardened. 'Come on, you sap, let's see the colour of your money. You can pay in gold dust, if you wish. Pay up, or quit wasting my time.'

Cal began to blush as he heard

giggles from the parlour. 'I ain't got no gold dust yet.' He stumbled away down the stairs. 'I'll come back when I'm rich.'

The redhead on the door wasn't smiling any more, either. In fact, she hit him on the head with her parasol. 'Clear off, cheapskate. What you trying to do, get me into trouble?'

'Dang me!' He hurried away. 'I ain't never heard of no places like that.'

A two-horse wagon with six men armed with shotguns and carbines was pulling away from the Wells, Fargo office. He guessed they were escorting gold some place, maybe down to California. Next door was the Miners' Exchange so the youth stepped inside.

A sign said, 'Gold Bought and Sold. Fair Rates.' A man was sitting behind an iron grille. 'What can I do for you?' he asked.

'Where do I go to dig up gold?'

'What?' he growled.

'Where's the best place to try my luck?'

'Try your luck? Pal, are you crazy? It's a bit late for that. What you gonna do? Tunnel three hundred vertical feet through the rock all on your own?'

'No, but I thought there were places you could scrape about on. A fella tol' me you can pick up nuggets.'

'Buster, he was pulling your leg. That's all over long ago. The big boys have taken over. They're looking for men along at the Mohawk Mine.' He rubber-stamped a chit and passed it through. 'Report there at six in the morning. You'll get four dollars a day.'

'The big boys? You mean the big mining companies? Ain't there anything else? I ain't gonna git rich on four dollars a day.'

A tall man in a caped greatcoat and wide-brimmed hat was standing in the office listening and gave a chuckle. 'You might be able to buy a small claim for five hundred dollars or so from some guy who's pulling out. But you're more'n likely to get gulled.'

'You mean it would probably be

played out? Worthless?'

'You got it. Or non-existent. Boy, you need to watch out in this town. There's a lot of conmen and two-timers around. Same applies to wimmin, too. All they're interested in is parting you from your cash.'

'I ain't got none so they're outa luck.' Cal looked a tad dumbfounded. 'Aw, well,' he said, waving the chit and turning to leave. 'Four dollars a day I guess it is.'

He was standing on the sidewalk wondering whether to spend what little he did have on coffee and cake when the stranger emerged from the exchange.

'Don't look so downhearted,' he said, taking Cal's arm. 'Let me treat you to this.' He ushered the youngster into the restaurant. 'I may have a proposition for you.'

'A proposition?' Cal wasn't sure he liked the sound of that. 'What sort of proposition?'

'Sit down. Have a slice of that chocolate cake you were eyeing. Waitress, two coffees.'

He was tall and emaciated. His hair was grey, greasy and thinning. It straggled down in old-frontier style to hang on his shoulders. Cal wondered why he was wrapped up as if it was mid-winter. The gent was suddenly racked by a cough and pulled out a 'kerchief. Cal noticed the blood specks. So that was why. He had consumption, was probably dying.

'The handle's Abe McLintock.' The stranger unbuttoned his greatcoat to reveal a sturdy Smith & Wesson handgun hitched to his belt. 'You interest me. You strike me as honest but naïve.'

Cal gripped his proffered hand. 'I'm Caleb Mitchell. I guess you people must get that impression. Just made a fool of myself in the Esmeralda. Thought it was a genuine hotel.'

'No, it's the best whorehouse in town. Sounds to me like you've got a lot to learn. That's why I'm interested in you. To me you're like a lump of virgin clay. I can help mould you.'

120

Cal didn't like the sound of that, either, but he was busy getting stuck into the chunk of cake which was delicious. 'Oh, yeah?' he mumbled.

'Yes, you see I'm the proprietor of The Grotto, down the street. It's a saloon and gambling house. I'm looking for someone to manage it for me. All the guys I know, they're sharp operators. I can't trust 'em.'

'You think you can trust me?'

'Yes.' Green eyes in a pallid, wearily-lined face, contemplated him. 'I do.'

'What would I have to do?'

'Supervise the games. Deal with troublemakers. Watch out for crooks and cheats.'

'But, that's crazy. I ain't never played cards.'

'What the hell did you do at home in the winter evenings?'

'I dunno, we generally read the Bible. No gambling, cussing, drinking of spirituous liquor was allowed where I come from.'

'A religious family? And you've

121

decided to get away and make your fortune. You ain't gonna save much on four dollars a day. You got a one-in-eight chance of getting killed down those mines, too.'

McLintock stirred his coffee, thoughtfully. 'You don't carry a gun, either. You got something against that, as well?'

'No, I left my rifle with my hoss. I can shoot.'

'I mean a sidearm. A man sure needs one in these parts. The whiskey's strong. Drunken arguments flare up all the time. Men round here ain't got nuthin' else to do on a Sunday 'cept kill each other.'

The older man laughed and slapped his shoulder. 'Don't look so alarmed. It ain't that bad.'

'So what are the odds on my staying alive in *your* establishment?'

'I can teach you to shoot.' McLintock whipped out the 'Wesson, spun it on a finger, pointed it at him, then returned it to the holster in one fluid movement. 'I used to be one of the best.'

'Aw, that's all very well, but it would take me years to learn all a gambler's tricks.'

'Not really. You seem an intelligent cuss. I'd give you a quick intensive course, see how you made out. If you couldn't cut the mustard then it would be no deal.'

'So, how much would you pay me?'

'A damn sight more than four dollars a day.'

'Thanks for the offer,' Cal said, as they left the restaurant. 'I just ain't planning on being some fast-gun gambling man, even if I could be. Looks like the mine for me.'

'Too bad, Cal. If you change your mind you know where to find me.'

'Yeah. OK.' Young Mitchell collected his horse and led him along to a livery run by a horse dealer called Garcia. There certainly seemed to be some nefarious-looking characters around. It was time for him to wise-up and be more on his guard. This wasn't Caliente. Already millions of dollars' worth of gold had been found beneath this town and it had lured bad hats and human vultures from all parts of the West. As security was tightened up many had fallen on hard times. The last thing he wanted was his horse stolen. That, his saddle and Winchester were the only valuable possessions he owned. He had heard there was no such animal as an *honest* horse dealer, but Nero should be safe enough in his stall at a dollar-a-night.

There was a three-storey, somewhat flimsy-looking structure, Brown's Hotel, opposite so he went inside. 'Is this a proper hotel?' Cal ventured. 'I mean, I just want a bed.'

Mr Brown smirked. 'That's all you'd be getting, son, for a dollar. Or one pinch of gold dust, whichever. Supper is fifty cents.'

'You've got a room?'

'We got two hundred of 'em. Was a time we were fully booked. But, yes, we got a few spare.'

When Cal had paid, the portly Brown

tossed him a moth-eaten blanket and pointed aloft. 'Number 69, top floor.'

'Don't I get a key?'

'A key? What for? This joint ain't named The Ritz. By the way, we'd appreciate it if you didn't wear your spurs in bed.'

Cal climbed up through a warren of small rooms, many apparently empty, their walls made of thin plywood, and found his. Four-feet-wide, it was bare but for an iron cot and a none-too-clean rolled-up mattress.

'Wow!' he exclaimed, peering out of the tiny window at the view. 'I ain't never had my own room afore. This is luxury!'

* * *

The Mohawk mine had a seam of gold, eight inches thick, that assayed $250,000 a ton, one of the richest pockets ever to be found in the United States, apart from Cripple Creek, Colorado. In fact, all of Goldfield's mines were similarly spectacular.

Naturally, the big money men had been quick to move in with specialist mining equipment. Most of Goldfield's mines were owned by absentee fat cats who leased them at a high return to mining companies. These professionals then dug frantically to get out all the gold they could before the leases expired. The system resulted in the heedless gutting of mines.

The Mohawk was no exception. It's superintendent pushed the miners to the limit, urging them to work harder and faster, unheeding of such fine ideas as health and safety rules. At Goldfield, $30 million of high grade ore was reaped over the years, but at what human cost was never revealed.

When Cal Mitchell reported for duty in the morning he was told that as he had no experience his pay would be only $3.50 a day. The older miners were surlily resentful of raw recruits. They slowed them down and were unwittingly dangerous. So, after Cal had been lowered down in a cage half-a-mile, it seemed, with a gang of them, he was put to the most menial back-breaking tasks, shovelling ore in the dusty gloom and hauling heavy tubs of it along the narrow passageways, aided by badly treated mules.

The miners worked in darkness all day from dawn to dusk. When Cal got back to his poky room he was too exhausted to do much more than lie on his bunk. On the fourth day he was handed a pick-axe, and told to crawl along a two-feet wide ledge and start hacking. Because of the steam heat most of the men worked naked, but for their boots, in such gold-face holes, for the drag of their sweat-wet garments hindered their movements. As a man was so confined he couldn't get a good swing of the pick. Cal discovered he had aches in muscles he didn't know he had. When he got back out of the hole he dragged his clothes back on.

At midday the miners were allowed a break to eat from their lunch pails. Cal

squatted on a rock beside a Cornishman who was devouring a curious
pasty, meat and parsnips in one end of
the pastry and apple in the other as a
dessert. The youth emptied sweat from
his boots and chewed on a bit of meat
jerky. In the flickering candlelight he
noticed that the Cornishman, Andy,
was filling the bottom of his lunchpail
with ore. 'Ain't that dishonest?' his
upbringing prompted him to say.

The dust-streaked faces of the other
miners glowered at him. 'What you
gonna do, sonny?' one snarled.
'Squeal?'

'It's our perk,' Andy explained. 'You
want some fat-arsed capitalist sitting in
his New York mansion to get it all?'

As the days wore on Cal noticed that
many of the men had pockets made of
long canvas tubes hung down their legs
inside their work trousers, or specially
made, many-pocketed vests they wore
under their shirts, or even double-
crowned hats where they secreted
nuggets of high-grade ore. Most took

out three or four pounds in weight a day, so much so that some staggered bandily under the strain.

What could Cal do but help himself to some, too? Otherwise he would have been treated as scum by his companions. And, anyway, it was true, they were the ones doing the work. This mountain belonged to the Lord, not some rich man in New York. Nonetheless, he felt a tad guilty about his perks.

Mostly the superintendent and his bully boys turned a blind eye when the miners lurched out of the cage with their heavy loads. If they had slammed down on the practice, known as high-grading, they would have had angry miners on a go-slow, or even out on strike for more pay. It was not until later years when they introduced pithead baths and made the men strip off and change their clothes, that they all but abolished the practice.

'What do I do with this stuff now?' Cal asked, as he trudged away one night with the Cornishman.

'Follow me. You could crush it, mix it with brass filings and spend it. But I get rid of it as fast as I can for cash.'

Andy led him in the dark to the office of a crooked assayer who quickly weighed their gold and paid in cash. It was worth about fifty per cent of the gold's true value, but that was the game.

'I sometimes make about a hundred and fifty dollars a month on top of my wage. Fair enough, ain't it, lover? Don't spend it all at once.' Andy, like many of the miners, lived in flimsy cabins they had built on the edge of town. 'Why don't you move in with me? I got plenty of room.'

Cal turned the offer down as politely as he could. He wasn't so sure about being called 'lover'. Although, perhaps it was just a quirk of Cornishmen's talk.

And, as he lay on his bunk waiting for another hellish day to begin, he wasn't sure he planned being a miner much longer. McLintock had told him he was a 'lump of virgin clay'. That was a bit odd, too. But maybe he would try being a gambler. It might be a more amenable way of making his fortune. He certainly needed to improve his shooting if he was to go back one day and face Houck and the Granger clan. And — it was his fervent main hope — take Modesty away and start a new life someplace.

It so happened the next day was Sunday so the miners had the day off. Most sat around town on the sidewalks, or poured into the saloons, gaming hells and red-light joints. Cal visited Nero and took him for a good long ride.

Garcia watched as he rubbed down the sweating stallion. 'How about I borrow him to cover my mares?' he asked, jerking a thumb at the horses in his corral out back.

'Don't folk gen'rally get paid for a stallion's services?' Cal was getting as dollar-conscious as all the other Gold-field folk.

'OK,' the dealer grinned. 'He gets free stall and feed.'

'How about five dollars a week on top?'

'You drive hard bargain.' Garcia peeled a five-buck note from a roll. 'OK. That your first week.'

'Looks like we're both working for our living,' Cal said, slapping the stallion's neck. 'Only you've got the better deal. Watch how you handle him. He only trusts me. He's got a killer kick.'

'Sure,' Garcia smiled. 'I know how to handle horses.'

'Well, you treat him right, or you'll answer to me.'

He had seen too many poor horses, their spirit totally broken, or even killed by cruel handling.

By chance, he was on his way to buy a chunk of pound cake and a coffee at the restaurant when he bumped into McLintock. 'Good God, Cal, you look a mess,' the emaciated gambler told him. 'Ain't you got any clean clothes for a Sunday?'

Cal tried, apologetically, to brush some of the dust from his dirt-stained and torn shirt and jeans, without much improvement. 'No, I ain't.'

'Well, I suggest you get some. You look like some tramp. You enjoying being a miner?'

'Not exactly enjoying, but I'm gittin' the hang of it. I've stuck it two weeks.'

'So?' A smile played on McLintock's lips as he stroked his thin moustache. 'You thought about my offer?'

'Yes, I have, sir.' On the spur of the moment Cal said, 'I'll take it.'

'You will? You sure?' In his caped greatcoat and wide-brimmed hat the older man was suddenly seized with another fit of coughing. He spat blood into the dust. 'Good. Because I might not have much time to teach you all I know.'

'So, when do I start?'

'Now. First we'll go get you some decent duds. You'll be needing a visit to the bath house, then a haircut. When you look half-presentable, we'll buy you a handgun and ride out to the tip where they chuck all the empty bottles. You'll be needing plenty of practice.'

8

McLintock marched Cal to the barber shop. 'Don't take too much off,' he instructed, as he sat and watched. 'The ladies like a lionesque mane. Just trim up and shape it.'

'What's it got to do with the ladies?' Cal asked, as the scissors snipped around his ears.

'If you're gonna run my casino you gotta look the part. If a man's attractive to the ladies it gives him an air of confidence. And if he's well turned out other men, the punters, respect him. So our next port of call is the tailor's.'

'I don't feel comfortable in this kinda gear,' Cal told him as he was measured for a two-piece suit in dove grey with silver lapel facings. 'I hope you ain't gonna turn me into some sorta popinjay.'

'Nothing but the best is good

enough.' McLintock pulled out a pouch of gold dust and paid for new socks, underwear, a pair of black, silver-enscrolled boots, brown twill riding pants and couple of blue woollen shirts. 'You can chuck that hat of yours in the trash bin and get yourself a new J.B.'

The casino owner removed with fastidious thumb and forefinger the discarded socks, shirt and jeans as Cal scrubbed himself in a hot tub in the bath house. He tossed them out of the window. 'You need to look smart even if you're dressed casual for riding,' he drawled. 'Regard yourself as a walking advertisement for my business.'

'Huh! Makes me sound like a tailor's dummy.' But Cal looked like a new man in the narrow-legged twill britches, blue shirt and loose tie. He bashed a couple of dents into the grey Stetson. 'I'll be glad when this looks more like my old one. How am I gonna pay you for all this?'

McLintock's eys twinkled. 'Don't worry about it. I'm taking a gamble making an investment in you. I expect to see a return.'

In his squeaky new boots Cal ambled with him along to Dan Travis's gun shop. 'You don't need nothing fancy, just a good solid side arm,' McLintock advised, as he examined a selection, holding each up to his ear, spinning the cylinders and testing the mechanism. He chose a Remington new model Army revolver, .44 calibre and a solid, tooled-leather gunbelt to fit it. 'How's that feel?'

Cal buckled the belt round his waist and took hold of the six-gun by its walnut grip. He tried pushing it in and pulling it out of the holster several times. 'OK.'

'You'll need to be faster than that. Keep the leather greased inside. Right, we'll head for the dump and see how you do.'

The emaciated McLintock might not look it, but in the past he had been a man it was not wise to cross, or come up against in a gun duel. Out on the edge of town he tossed bottles into the air, watched, astutely, as Cal tried to take them out. Of six bottles the youth only managed to hit two.

'You're gonna have to do better than that. Watch me. Start throwing, fast as you like.' McLintock unbuttoned his greatcoat, drew the Smith & Wesson and demolished all six in the sky. 'Mind you, I don't have to cock this which helps. Don't use your thumb, try cocking your hammer with the palm of your left hand. Fan it.'

'Maybe if I had my holster on the left hip and used the cross-hand draw like you.'

'Don't try to run before you can walk, Cal.' McLintock smiled at him. 'Don't worry. You come here every day and practise, you'll soon improve. Now for the hardest test.'

'What's that?'

'The cards. We'll see how you deal.'

★ ★ ★

Most of the boom town's luxuries had to be hauled up steep, winding trails from California and a mule train was clipping into Goldfield, the first ten pairs packing two kegs of whiskey apiece, the others carrying flour. An ancient muleskinner, covered in dust, yelled to them to halt outside The Grotto.

'Howdy, Sam,' McLintock called. 'Roll 'em in and I'll settle up with you. This here's Cal. He may well be dealing with you in future.'

All the windows were curtained and candles illuminated the big hall in which, being Sunday, there were men shoulder to shoulder at the bar, or crowded around the green-baize tables. Conversation was surprisingly muted as eyes concentrated on the game. Most knew that any rowdiness would result in a permanent ban from this haven.

'Go do your cussin', fightin' and carousin' some place else,' McLintock would tell any he had to eject.

Cal was surprised to see three gaudily dressed young women dealing at the tables. One, powdered and perfumed, blonde hair coiled up on top of her head, had a cigarette dangling from her painted lips.

'That's Cincinnatti Sal,' the casino owner remarked. 'She's chief croupier. Used to be a schoolmarm.'

'Why not men dealers?'

'I don't trust 'em. The gals bring in the men. Kinda dazzle the poor suckers. The guys try to impress 'em, don't like to lose face, or pull out. They wildly wager more so they won't look like they lack pluck.'

'What are those counters they're playing with?'

McLintock eyed him, curiously. 'Jeez, is this the first time you've been in a gambling den? These are chips. They pay for 'em generally in gold dust up at the bar where those scales are. Pug will show you how to weigh dust.'

'Who's he?'

'That bruiser with the broken nose behind the bar. He used to be a bare-knuckle fighter. I gave him the job when he came outa the pen. He's solid as a rock. Thick as one, too, you know, punchy.'

Pug, his muscles bulging beneath a striped shirt, gave them a toothless grin and plonked a bottle and two tumblers in front of them. 'Who's this, boss?'

'Our new apprentice, Cal Mitchell. Pug's my second-in-command. He'll advise you, but you only take orders from me.' McLintock filled his tumbler to the brim with whiskey. 'The first drink's on the house to all customers. Fancy a snifter?'

'No, I don't drink. Well, that red beer's OK.'

'Good. Stick to that. You got to keep your brain alert. Too many men are slaves to corn lightning. You think it won't getcha, but it always does.'

As if to prove his point he went into one of his spasms of coughing, expectorating accurately at a brass spitoon. When he had recovered he nodded at the roulette table.

'We take most of our cash on the wheel. You put your chips on your chosen number. There's thirty-six to bagck, with a zero and double zero. No

140

late calls. Lucky Lucy there's raking in the chips that feller lost.'

'What's going on under that painting of a tiger?'

'The Bengal tiger? That's faro. Pegleg Jenny — she lost her foot from frostbite — is shuffling the pack an' placing it face up in the deal box. Now she's flipping 'em out. You back any card to win or lose. If you win you're paid off in even money. Even stevens. It's simple. There's some other ramifications Jenny'll explain.'

'Why is that table empty?'

'The blackjack game's out of operation. Vera's off-duty. She'll start again at midnight. We never close. You get twelve hours on and twelve off. I might deal it myself in a little while.'

McLintock led him into a back area where games were going on. 'It's poker and three card monte in here. High rollers. All drinks to them are free. Those boys have been at it since last night.'

'Who are the guys in the plug hats?'

Cal eyed the dudes, some had frock coats draped over the backs of their chairs. They had diamond stickpins in cravats and gold watch chains draped across the bellies of their fancy vests, a marked contrast to the roughly attired miners.

'They are what we call the gentlemen of the fraternity. Professionals. They don't like the term gambler. It's more of a science to them. Treat 'em with respect, but don't let 'em hoodwink you. If there's any hanky-panky, you politely and quietly ask them to leave. We avoid gunplay if possible. Pay 'em off and they'll go. They'll move on to Virginia City or Santa Fe or Denver, try their tricks there.'

'What sort of tricks?'

'Hell, you are raw, aincha? Let's see now. They'll crimp cards, sandpaper them, mark them with their finger nails, keep a pin in a bandaged finger to punch holes in them. Why, some even try keeping an ace up the sleeve of their coat. Others might be in cahoots with a waitress, who gives him a wink or tweak of her ear as she serves his opponent and sees his hand. I estimate we get taken for ten thousand or so dollars a year,' McLintock explained, ruefully. 'I aim to cut that back. That'll be part of your job.'

'Whew! This is making my head spin trying to remember just the basics.'

'Don't worry, you'll pick it all up. If you suspect cheating the first thing to do is open a new deck. We call that 'old-decking' a player out of the game. You see those two miners playing chuck-a-luck at the bar? You should keep an eye on 'em to make sure one ain't using loaded dice, playing Greek shots. You can bet he'd have the nerve to squawk if we showed him the door. Let's go into my office.'

It was more like a parlour with an oriental carpet on the floor, big carved-wood desk, maroon velvet *chaise-longue*, brass oil lamp with cranberry-coloured bowl, logs in the fireplace ready for winter, an iron, Yale lock safe, wardrobe with bevelled mirror, oil paintings and antique flintlocks decorating the walls.

McLintock removed his topcoat, relaxed in a padded swivel chair behind the desk and slapped down a pack of cards. 'These are your new friends. You'll have to get to know 'em intimately.' With expert legerdemain he flicked them out in a row and back up his sleeve like some conjuror on stage. He sent the cards in an arc from one hand to the other, fanned them out to point out the picture cards, ace and joker in the pack. Then placed them neatly before Cal. 'Let's see you do that.'

'You're joking.' He fumblingly tried to shuffle the deck, dropping one in the process. 'Hot damn!'

'Relax. Take your time. Always stay cool-headed.' But McLintock sighed and shook his head. 'You sure got a lot of work to do, Cal. You take that pack to your room and practise. You've got sensitive fingers. Don't worry, boy. I'll make a gambler and shootist outa you.'

* * *

Modesty Mitchell was aware that something had changed inside her. As the days wore on she became convinced that she had conceived. It was a fearsome shock to the girl. 'I must have been mad,' she whispered to herself as memories of the torrid afternoons of lovemaking with her brother returned to her. 'Just what did I expect? I should have known.'

The shame for a girl from a religious family would be almost too much to bear. Her nights, too, were haunted by stories remembered of incestuous women producing children with two heads or other ways deformed. Perhaps these were old wives' tales but they frightened her.

'What's wrong with you?' Martha demanded one day in the dairy cave. 'Why you moping and looking so miserable? Is it what I think it is?'

Modesty nodded, wide-eyed. 'What can I do?'

'There's ways.' Her mother screwed her with gimlet eyes. 'We're lucky ye've found out early. It don't show yet. God knows what your father will do when he knows. I fear he might well throw you out of the house.'

Modesty looked even more scared. 'What would I do then?'

'What, indeed?' Martha looked even more gaunt and old as she considered the possibilities. Her belief forbade that a foetus should be aborted. Many such abandoned girls ended their days in a whorehouse. It was all that was left to them. 'We'll have to find you a husband.'

'A husband?' Modesty repeated with dismay. 'I don't want a husband. There's nobody I could — !

'You're a good-lookin' gal. Surely some young feller must have made eyes at you. What about that Josh?'

'Josh? But he's a Granger.'

'I know. It will half-kill your father. But I've seen Josh buzzin' about you. He's a big, healthy, strong, hard-working man. The only one of the Grangers with a shred of decency. It's time we built bridges. Seems to me he's

146

the only candidate.'

'But,' Modesty protested, 'I don't like him like that.'

'Somebody in your position cain't be choosy. You gotta get to like him. There ain't no buts, girl.'

Modesty was silent, swallowing this unpalatable prospect. Josh was OK, but he was so huge, bearded, a matt of black hair covering his chest. She remembered Cal's slim whipcord muscular body and sighed. That was all in the past. It had to be. She had no choice.

'Don't look so down. Try to look your cheerful self. Your father is going away to Salt Lake City for a week or so. This is your opportunity. I'll take you into Temperance. If we meet Josh you be nice to him, smile, laugh, tease him with them dark eyes of yourn. But never give him a hint of what's been done to you.'

'I'm not that stupid, Mother. If he knew he'd drop me like a hot brick.'

Her parents had assumed that Cal

had raped her on that one occasion with little encouragement from her. Modesty had felt guilty not to tell them the truth. But since Cal had shot Aaron down like that it had destroyed everything. How quickly red-hot love had turned into intense hatred. Now she had to think of herself and the child to be.

The shock of being left alone, all three of his sons gone, just a barren wife and a wanton daughter remaining, had driven Gideon Mitchell to the verge of despair. Who would look after them in their old age? They would be destitute when they were no longer able to work.

But he was not that old, in his fifties, a virile, property-owning man. He had made a decision that brightened the future. He would go to Salt Lake City and find a new wife, maybe buy one with what savings he had. Perhaps the Lord would give him another chance. Gideon would sow his seed and procreate. He rather liked the idea and made haste to be on his way, unaware of what was going on behind his back.

★ ★ ★

To Modesty it was as if it was suddenly foreordained. When her mother drove her into Temperance who should be there but Joshua Granger picking up some sacks of grain. He naturally offered to help load some for them. Modesty smiled and flirted, as she had been bid, and Martha invited Josh to call at the ranch one evening when he was free and take some refreshment with them. Hearing that Gideon was away, Josh jumped at the chance. He donned his best church suit and hat and rode over the next afternoon. After some small talk and a glass or two of non-alcoholic cordial he sat on the veranda with Modesty. Just the rustle of her black silk mourning dress, the movement of her slim body, the look in her lustrous eyes, inflamed him, set his whole body pounding. As darkness descended he gripped her dainty hand with his hairy-backed paw, went down on one knee. 'Modesty, I know this must come as a surprise, but I want you . . . I want you to marry me.'

'I ain't having that Mitchell bitch as a daughter-in-law,' the lawyer, Isaac, shouted when the news was broken to him. 'Are you mad? She's making a fool out of you. A bigger fool than you already look.'

'She won't be your daughter-in-law. You ain't my father,' Joshua roared. 'I love Modesty and she loves me, so I'd warn you not to insult her or me again. Who the hell you think you are? You don't own me.'

'I've got power of attorney over my late brother's estate and the honour of making sure his wishes are carried out. You take up with a Mitchell you'll get nothing. None of us Grangers will want to have anything to do with you.'

'I'll fight you in court. I'm entitled to my section of land. It's a natural right. All this feuding, anyway, I'm sick of it.

What's it all for? I wanted nothing to do with the burning of their ranch, the killing of Jed. What had he ever done to us? You were behind that attack, Isaac, you and your hired gun. You think you can do what you damn well like up in this corner of the country, run rough-shod over everybody. I'll remind you we live in the United States. If the authorities ever found out what you done, Big Shot Isaac, you'd be for the high jump.'

'All right, simmer down.' Captain Granger quickly changed his tune. 'Perhaps it's not a bad idea. I spoke rashly. She's certainly a good-looking hussy. It's a shock to me, that's all. I'm only thinking of your future, Joshua. I fear you may regret this decision. But seems your mind's made up. It'll certainly be one in the eye for Gideon Mitchell.'

'Her mother, Martha, says he prob-ably won't give his blessing, but I don't care. I'll marry Modesty without it. So, don't worry, you won't have to meet him at the wedding.'

'Good. In that case I'll make no objection. As the oldest son you are entitled to the best section.'

'Yeah, well, I've had my eye on that stretch along the river. It'd suit us.'

'No problem.' Isaac forced a smile and offered his hand. 'Congratulations, Josh. When's the big day to be?'

'Soon as possible.' Joshua beamed. 'I just cain't wait. I've been thinking, maybe the week after next.'

'Damn fool!' the lawyer said, as he watched Joshua ride out of town. 'Strikes me it's that conniving li'l bitch and her mother who've been doing the thinking. It's pretty obvious what's going on.'

James Houck chuckled as he stood by his side outside his office. 'So what you gonna do about it?'

'What can I do? He threatened me, talked about going to the authorities. You know I've got political ambitions in this state. It would ruin me.'

Houck chuckled again and scratched his unshaven jaw. 'Maybe I should ride out to their ranch, too, while Gideon Mitchell's away, have a word with Modesty.'

'No, James. I don't want any more trouble.'

'No? What a pity you say that. I got a score to settle with that li'l wildcat.'

9

Two years later.

A lithely muscled, seventeen-year-old Japanese labourer, Higo Chaguro, swung precariously back and forth in a basket as he was lowered over a yawning precipice amid the highest peaks of the Sierra Nevada. Below him hundreds of Chinese coolies were toiling with shovels and barrows to clear a way for the Central Pacific railroad. His bossman bellowed through a megaphone up to him to say where he wanted holes to be chiselled, black powder charges to be placed.

Higo had never dreamed there could be such an expanse of space, such a farflung landscape of mountains and wilderness. He had volunteered for the task although he knew that many of their number had already fallen to their deaths or horrifying injuries. As the

154

basket suddenly gave a stomach-churning lurch to one side he hung on to the rope to try to steady himself. He was both frightened and excited by the risky operation. The rope was a pendulum swinging him between life or death.

Finally the charges were set and he was hauled upwards to safety. 'Well, done, lad.' The old man, Junzo Negato, caught him as he leapt from the basket's trestle crane on to the clifftop. 'It takes some nerve to do that. Come on, we've got to get out of here.'

The fuse wires were already being rolled out and the plungers manned. Down below the Chinese were scurrying to evacuate the area. The ground trembled and the huge bulk of the precipice from which Higo had been suspended collapsed in a roar of exploded dust and tumbling rocks.

Soon the bossman was shouting to the coolies to get back in and start clearing the rubble, hitting out at any laggardly ones with his swinging club.

155

They would be given no rest until dusk.

The logistics of the greatest feat of engineering ever attempted in America were mind-boggling. The plan to push a railroad through this wall of mountains from California to the East had been the brainchild of four Sacramento merchants.

For years now they had been raising investments, fighting for government backing, even before a route had been surveyed. To avoid high labour cost 12,000 Chinese and hundreds of Japanese had been imported. Six locomotives, iron rails, girders, and machinery had been shipped from New York all the way round Cape Horn, a voyage of eight months, and hauled for miles up the mountain tracks by oxen teams. A dozen sawmills had been set up to provide the timber for trestle bridges and ties, and snow sheds roofed with iron had had to be built to protect the track.

The past winter had been the most horrendous Higo had known, the labourers working on and on through blizzards of ice. At one section they had had to shovel through sixty feet depth of snow for nine miles merely to get to the road bed. Many froze to death cowering in their flimsy shelters through the long nights.

Now, four years of grading, tunnelling through solid rock and track-laying, a task that many pooh-poohed as impossible, was nearing victorious conclusion. Soon, it was rumoured, they would be entering Nevada and crossing a flat stretch of alkali desert for many miles, although the scarcity of water for both engines and humans would have to be faced. But it was early summer and spirits had soared.

'Why you risk your life on that rope I cannot imagine,' old Mr Negato said, as, at the end of the day they made their way wearily back to their bivouac.

Young Higo stroked his long black hair away from his graceful features. 'Somebody's got to do it. Better me than you. Anyway, the few cents extra they pay me danger money comes in handy.'

★ ★ ★

Higo had never intended to be a railroad worker. It was news of the California goldrush that had prompted him to head for America. As a twelve-year-old boy, Higo had become servant to a samurai warrior. He had learned to dress him in his armour, to hand him his sword according to exact pageantry, to groom his stallion. He had never been taught how to use the samurai sword for he was of too low a caste. But he had watched carefully and, when his master was absent, practised the moves and ventured to ride the stallion, although fearful that he might be caught. He became familiar with all the pageantry, the religious meditation, the jousting and fighting of the knights.

But evil days had come to Japan with the arrival of the foreigners, the

158

Americans and British. They were afraid of the power of the samurai and persuaded the emperor in Tokyo to disband them. So it came about that the samurai were outlawed. Higo, who had hoped to stay in his lord's household, found himself, aged sixteen, out of work and forced to go back to his village, Fukio, to work in the rice fields.

However, poverty forced him to leave his village, walk to far off Yokohama. Matters did not improve there. He hired himself out as a porter on the dock-side, staggering all day under huge loads. The lowest of the low. At nights he slept in a packing case.

One day he paused to listen to the words of a *tojin-san*, a foreigner, on the quayside. He was lured by his blandishments to give him the little bundle of cash he had carefully saved for his return home. No, the man said: he could make a fortune in California picking gold nuggets up from the ground. He offered Higo the privilege of a berth on his dilapidated sailing barque. First-class accommodation would be provided. Well, these Americans certainly had a sense of humour if that was their idea of first class.

Higo had been jammed into a foetid hold packed with other men. In that creaking hole they had scarcely room to stretch their legs. And what a frightening vastness it was, the Pacific Ocean, on which the fragile craft tossed and heaved to every wave. Higo had come to know the true meaning of the saying, 'A sea voyage is an inch from Hell.'

Eventually they sailed into San Francisco harbour, 'the promised land' and Higo marvelled at the tall-masted clippers, the motley array of craft, the crush of people on the harbourside, the babel of tongues, the screams and cacophony coming from quayside taverns. The men were led through the dilapidated tenements of China Town, crushed into filthy attic rooms and warned not to go out for the neighbourhood was a nest of opium cellars, gambling dens and Chinese brothels

160

protected by bloodthirsty tongs.

The *tojin-san*, the next day, had offered them a chance to earn good money. He herded them on to a steam ferry to take them across the bay to Vallejo. They were loaded into a goods van. Before the door slid closed on them Higo caught his last glimpse of the *tojin-san* counting some greenback dollars he had been paid by the guard. They were later informed this was their first month's wages claimed for their delivery fee.

The locomotive, drawing supplies and girders, went rattling on its way, through Sacramento and Dutch Flats to begin its climb huffing and puffing up the ascent. It was on the journey that Higo met the old man, Junzo Negato, who laughed merrily when the young Japanese told him he planned to save a cash stake and go gold mining.

'The rush was over years ago,' he cried. 'Big mining companies have taken over. There are a few hopefuls re-sifting the old placers but they barely make enough to buy their rotgut whiskey.'

When the train stopped one night at a mining town called Gold Gulch Junzo told him they had time to stretch their legs and take a look. The mountainside had been devastated, washed away by the powerful hydraulic jets now in use by the companies. There were a few desolate cabins and grog shops where they could see through the open doors bearded, dusty men making merry.

Junzo pointed to a scrawled notice pinned to the timber wall outside. 'No dogs or Chinese.' He sighed. 'I do not think they would welcome us Japanese either.'

Mr Negato had worked on the railroad from early days, saved a good sum, planning to return to his homeland, but had lost most of it in a 'Frisco gambling den. He spoke good English, knew the ropes and seemed to have taken a liking to Higo. He proved a useful and cheerful companion.

Thus it was that Higo joined the

railroad company, was issued with a wooden tag that he had to wear around his neck for identification, and joined in the great endeavour. He was wary at first of the Chinese, traditional enemies, who, he had been led to believe were cruel barbarians. But they seemed to be polite, hard-working, expert cooks, even their secret societies motivated to help one another.

Thus they laboured on, battling heat and thirst, across the desert, urged to go ever faster, and Higo was among the gang of eight men handling all the iron rails who laid ten miles of track in one day, the greatest feat of railroad-building on record, so that in May, 1869, the first Union Pacific locomotive could steam into Promontory Point, Utah, to come nose to nose with the engine of the Central Pacific. The latter had come all the way from Chicago, but their top gang had only managed eight miles on their best day.

The workers were herded to one side as top-hatted big wigs posed for photographers and the last spike, the Golden Spike, was hammered home. His pay in the pouch on his belt, the bare-legged Higo, in his baggy loin-cloth, sandals and padded jacket, clothes he had worn since leaving home, grinned at Mr Negato. 'What do we do now?'

'Most of the workers are being shipped back to Sam Francisco,' he replied. 'But there is talk of a man seeking workers to build a branch line to go far to the south of here. It might be worth staying on.'

'Where will it go to?' Higo wondered, peering through the fringe of his thick hair at the bleak horizon.

'Goldfield. A town where they have many rich mines.'

'Why not?' Higo shouted, jubilantly. 'It will be an adventure. We, too, will get rich.'

But it would be an adventure they would both soon bitterly regret.

★ ★ ★

That the work would be hard and dangerous was not unanticipated. The first death on the railroad came quickly. A crane tipped out of true, a solid girder slipped and slid to trap beneath it a Japanese boy, Nanuki. 'Hold on,' Higo shouted, as he gritted his teeth, exerted all his strength to try to lift the girder. He braced his thighs, the veins in his forehead and biceps bulged. But his fingers began to slip. The terrified face of Nanuki, a boy of fifteen, looked up at him. He did not want to die. Slowly, inevitably, the girder pressed down. Higo had to jump clear to avoid being crushed himself. Nanuki screamed. Blood was gushing from his eyes, his nose, his mouth, his ears. Soon he ceased writhing. He was dead.

Even the boss man's face paled. Big Jim Hagerty gasped out, 'Enough to make a man bring up his breakfast.'

'Come on, get back to work,' his bullying foreman, Bill Somers, shouted, but the Japanese labourers demanded time to give the boy a burial. They bade the boy's spirit safe journey back to the land of their ancestors.

From the start Hagerty had warned them what to expect. Their meagre allowance of rice and dried fish would be docked from their pay.

'But what will our pay be?' Junzo Negato had asked.

'We'll have to work that out. Depends how hard you Japs work,' Hagerty growled. 'Meantime ye'll be issued with tokens to exchange for rations. You're allowed one canteen of water a day. Water's a precious commodity out here in the desert. Anybody disobeys the rules gets severely punished.'

'The dumb shits ain't understood a word,' Somers sneered. 'You're wasting your breath, boss.'

'Sir, there is no need to insult us,' Mr Negato objected. 'I will explain your request.'

'It ain't a request.' Hagerty, in his slouch hat and dusty suit, scowled at them. 'It's an order. If you don't like it I can tell you, you got a long walk home.'

'They ain't likely to argue.' Somers' sidekick, Luke Spence, was a lanky, sharp-faced Texan, attired in range leathers, a greasy Stetson on his head. He slapped the Paterson six-gun pig-stringed to his thigh. 'I'll make sure of that.'

From the start, the burly Somers, in a battered derby and dirt-brown top-coat, waded into them with his billystick, cursing them, and shouting that they should work harder. The small gang of Japanese labourers toiled from dawn to dusk, hauling rocks, dragging panniers of soil to build the track across the vast expanse of scrub.

'America is not as I expected it to be,' Higo Chaguro murmured as they squatted with their starvation diet in the rocks by the flickering camp-fire. 'This is a death railroad.'

'Nothing in life is as we expect it to be,' Mr Negato replied. 'We must persevere.'

Among them was an old man of

wrinkled brow, skinny bowed legs and sad eyes, Mr Oshuko, but what made Higo's heart leap was the sight of his young daughter, a Japanese girl in traditional dress. Her name was Tama, meaning jewel.

When he looked at her it was as if time had stood still and he was back in his own land amid the whispering bamboo groves, the interlacing boughs of hemlocks, the whistling calls of the woodbirds.

'Tell me, sir, what brings you to this land?' young Higo enquired for it was impolite to speak directly to the girl.

'When our samurai were banned, not even allowed to carry swords, we went to the city but were forced to live under most repugnant conditions,' the old man replied. 'We took ship to this lost and sorry land.'

'That has been the same experience of many of us,' Mr Negato remarked. 'We thought it would be good.'

'There must be a good place here in which we could settle.' He stared at

Tama, her almond-shaped eyes, her sweet, maidenly face, her hair, shiny black as a raven's wing, her slim body beneath the folds of her gown. 'Somewhere we can make a new life for ourselves.'

'If only we could find such a place,' she replied. 'Mother died on the ship and was cast into the waves. I am the only one father has to look after him.'

It pained Higo to see her being forced to toil with them under the harsh sun through the long days, her gown becoming dusty and torn, and he often tried to help her. A strong unspoken bond was formed between them. He longed to propose marriage to her. But what could he offer?

When her father expired from heat exhaustion, simply lay down and died, she was obviously stricken. But he was not the only one who tried to comfort her. A big, ham-thighed Japanese, the size of a sumo wrestler, Kantaro, was also smitten by Tama and persistently moved in on her. He was like some clumsy bumble bee buzzing about her, pushing Higo out of the way.

'You are not alone now,' Higo told Tama. 'I will look after you.'

'Pah,' Kentaro grunted. 'She needs a real man like me.'

Higo's English had improved under Mr Negato's tuition and it was obvious from what he overheard that the guards and their bossman also had eyes for the slender Japanese girl, but they were speaking about her crudely and offensively.

'Be warned,' Higo shouted, wagging a finger at them. 'You keep away from girl.'

The Texan, Luke Spence, cackled lecherously, pulled out his six-gun and threatened him. 'You gonna argue with this? Get back in line.'

That morning Spence and Somers suddenly caught hold of Higo, dragging him to Jim Hagerty, accusing him of stealing more than his share of water.

'That's a lie!' Higo protested, but they had tight hold of him, thrusting

him into an iron animal cage no   h
than two feet high.   t

'He's got to be punished,' Ha
shouted, leaving the Japanese y
trapped on his knees, without a ha
the baking noon sun. 'You others
back to work. Not you!' He pointed
Tama. 'I need to talk to you.'

The only two other Americans, the
engineer and his stoker, had taken their
locomotive back along the track to pick
up supplies. Higo twisted his neck and
saw Spence and Somers escorting the
work gang along the track to hack a way
through a ravine. Hagerty had hold of
Tama's arm and was dragging her into
his tent. Somers and Spence were
hurrying back to join them, evil grins
on their faces as they passed him.

The tent was five feet high with a tin
chimney from a stove poking through
the roof. Inside, Hagerty would plan
the railroad route, eat heartily, drink his
whiskey and sleep on his cot during the
hottest part of the day. Now Higo could
hear the raucous laughter of him and

is cronies as they got drunk. Suddenly here was a high-pitched scream and Higo's whole body tensed with fear. 'Tama!'

What were they doing to her? He hardly dare imagine. It must have been the longest hour of his life as he knelt cramped in the scorching heat, his head spinning, his heart aching, as he heard more laughter, more screams.

Then there was silence. Even more agonizing than the cursing and laughter. Eventually Spence stepped out, doing up his flies, followed by the red-faced Somers looking mightily pleased with himself. They trudged past him, back to the railroad gang.

Higo passed out in the heat. When he came to it was dusk and he was being dragged out of the cage and over to the cowed Japanese. 'What have you done with her?' he pleaded, through cracked, parched lips.

But when Somers brought Tama from the tent and pushed her, contemptuously, into their company, Higo had no need to ask again. Tama sat, her eyes downcast, her legs drawn up, obviously in pain, but mostly shattered by the shame of having her precious maidenhood taken by force by these pigs. They could not be called men.

Higo could barely stetch out his legs or get to his feet. 'Take it easy,' Mr Negato cautioned. 'These men have guns. There is nothing we can do.'

Kentaro, his belly hanging over his cotton pants, suddenly picked up an iron spike and waving it, roaring like a raging bull, raced towards the tent. '*Damuraisu!*' he screamed as Hagerty stepped from the tent, but before he could smash his skull with the spike a shot crashed out and he was brought rolling to the ground.

Luke Spence stood over Kentaro, his smoking Paterson in his fist, and finished him with a bullet between the eyes.

Hagerty strode over to the Japanese. 'Any of you lot get any ideas like that you can see what you'll get,' he shouted. 'You can bury him over in the rocks.'

When they were gone Higo, lying in the darkness, hardly able to move, hissed at Tama, 'I will avenge you.' But she would not meet his eyes, gently sobbing where she knelt. In the morning they found her crushed, lifeless body. Tama had climbed to the rim of the ravine cliff and hurled herself off. Rather than face dishonour she had chosen death.

'Four of us dead now,' Negato shouted at Hagerty. 'Are you satisfied?'

'Never heard of any law aginst killin' Japs,' Hagerty drawled.

'Poor Kentaro.' Junzo Negato sighed as his people returned to toiling like ants, swinging sledgehammers to crush rocks, using shovels to flatten the bed. 'His was the same resentfulness that animated the misguided patriots of Satsuma when they fought the Allied fleet at Kagoshima.'

The gang struggled to lay more rails. Their hammers rang out in unison.

'*Clang! Clang! Clang!*' Higo didn't know about resentfulness. There was more of a burning fury in him as he waited his chance. Luke Spence was sitting on his mustang watching proceedings and cackled as the rotund Somers cracked his billy across Higo's bent back. 'That's the way. Show the idle bastard who's boss.'

It was the last straw for Higo. He swung his shovel and hit the foreman a blow across his chest, then back again cutting the edge into his arm, making him drop the stick. Somers howled his surprise, backing away, nursing his bleeding bicep.

Spence scoffed, sardonically. 'You need any help? Cain't you take him?'

For reply the foreman snatched up a piece of discarded chain, winding it around his fist and swinging it. 'Come on, Jap.' He beckoned with his free hand. 'Come and try me.'

Higo had more of a spring in his step by now and eyed the two men cautiously as Spence jumped down to

175

join the fight. In his village Higo and his friends had eagerly practised the ancient art of unarmed combat, ju-jitsu, devised by peasants in the far off past to protect themselves from bandits. He was no grand master, but . . .

He ducked as he saw Somers' snarling face and the iron chain whistled over his head. His return swipe of the shovel caught the foreman in the side and bowled him over. The shovel slipped from his grasp and went with him.

Higo turned as Spence kicked a spurred boot at him, viciously. He caught the ankle, twisted, and he, too, went rolling. 'Oh, so it's like that, is it?' the Texan sneered, picking himself up out of the dust.

Higo balanced on the balls of his sandalled feet, his palms half-closed, prepared for them. But the burly foreman ran in from behind and snaked the chain around his throat, pulling it tight, half-choking him. He jabbed an elbow into Somers' fat gut, broke away and punched his fist into Spence's face as he tried to grapple with him.

'He's asking for another dose of the cage.' Spence charged back in, swinging haymakers that Higo dodged. He kicked out and caught the Texan in the temple, dislodging his Stetson. But now Somers was thrashing him with the chain. Higo saw red, caught hold of one end jerked the foreman to him, kneeing him in the groin. He wound the chain around his tormentor's throat and jerked him back against a rock. He exerted pressure harder and harder until he heard Somers' windpipe crack and he went limp.

He let him fall.

'You've killed him! cried the astonished Luke Spence. He hauled out his heavy revolver. 'Pretty nimble on your feet, eh? Let's see if you're fast enough to dodge a bullet.'

Higo looked into the deathly hole of the Paterson and knew he didn't have a chance. There was a burst of fire and smoke as the gun exploded and he hurled himself to one side. At the same moment Mr Negato smashed a rock against the Texan's head, felling him.

But Spence wasn't done yet. He rolled over and came up. The revolver exploded again and Junzo Negato gasped out as blood flowered from his chest. It was Higo's turn to be astonished. He knelt and closed his friend's eyes then snatched up an iron spike. The Texan was having trouble: his gun had jammed. Higo dived at him and stuck the spike hard into Spence's jugular so that his blood spouted like a faucet. Now three men sprawled dead in the dust, the flies already homing in on them.

Big Bill Hagerty had been busy with his theodolite surveying the track. When he heard the gunshots he ran towards his tent. Higo knew he was going for his rifle. He needed to get away fast. But if he was to escape he would need money. He kneeled over Somers and pulled a leather pouch from his coat pocket. It contained silver and gold coin. Spence had a roll of green bills in his shirt pocket. Higo tucked them into his belt.

A rifle shot cracked out and a bullet spurted dust by his feet. 'Here!' he cried to the watching labourers, tossing the pouch to them. 'Back wages. Share it.'

He had no time to lose. He leaped on to the mustang as another bullet tore through the sleeve of his padded jacket. He snatched up the reins, kicked in his heels and cried, 'Hagh!' He went galloping away along the ravine as more slugs buzzed past his ears like angry bees. Then he was out on to the plain and free to go charging away in the direction the railroad was headed. Goldfield!

10

Modesty was out in the yard helping her black maid, Cindy, hang out diapers and sheets to dry. Up in the sky a kite was hovering watching its prey. Instead of her spirit soaring at the sight she felt more like one of the rabbits cowering in the grass below.

'Why do I feel so down?' she sighed. 'I should thank my lucky stars. I've got a lovely baby boy, this safe, comfortable house to live in, my health and strength, and yet — I feel imprisoned on this ranch.'

'Aw,' Cindy consoled. 'Lots of wimmin feel down when they've had a chile. Maybe yo' jest too wild. Yo' got a good husband. What you 'plainin' 'bout?'

'Yes, I guess I have.' Modesty heard the thud of hoofs approaching across the grassy plain. 'And here he comes.'

Whooping and shouting, Josh Granger

and his brothers came galloping up to the front of the ranch house. Modesty frowned to see that his uncle Isaac and Sheriff Houck were along. 'I guess they'll be wanting coffee and eats,' she said, returning, somewhat reluctantly to the kitchen.

'We sure made them pilgrims run,' the barrel-chested Josh shouted, as he led the men in to join her. He slapped his horny hand hard on her rump and roared with laughter. 'They got a nerve, movin' in on a good bit of grass.'

Modesty flinched at his touch. She hated her husband slapping at her like she was one of his cows. 'You didn't kill anybody, did you?'

'Nah! We didn't need to,' Noah shouted. 'We ran 'em off back to where they come from like a herd of stinkin' sheep.'

'If they'd offered to pay rent it might have been different,' the lawyer remarked. 'But they thought they could have land for free.'

The boys clattered chairs around the

kitchen table. James Houck took a seat and watched Modesty through his dark, hooded eyes as he lit a cheroot. 'If we strung a couple of 'em up it would deter others from trying the same stunt,' he drawled.

Modesty had asked Joshua not bring him here. Houck's evil strength always disturbed her. So far she had evaded his clutches, but when her husband wasn't around he was always trying to touch her, or making some insolent remark. If she complained, Josh just shrugged and said, 'Aw, he's all right.'

Cindy at the stove was busy tossing pancakes and Modesty was clattering wooden platters on to the table for the boys. As she leaned past Houck his strong right hand pressed her side through her blouse. She brushed him away. 'Don't touch me,' she hissed.

Josh had gone outside to wash up under the tap so his absence prompted Houck to try his tricks. 'Ya know ya love it,' he taunted.

'How's my nephew li'l Dan today?'

Ephraim hollered.

Modesty had just breast-fed him. 'He's sleeping. So I'd appreciate it if you boys didn't make so much noise.'

As she fetched cutlery from the dresser and stepped back across the stone-flagged floor Houck scooped his boot beneath her loose-swinging skirt and hooked it up high. The men all guffawed at the sight of her shapely bare legs.

Modesty spun around and slapped Houck hard across his face. 'Any more,' she warned, 'and you'll regret it, you pig.'

Houck's apelike nostrils and lips spread in a grin. 'I'll remember that.'

But the sheriff was in the mood for mischief. 'How old's the kid now? Eighteen months? Don't it seem odd to you boys that this Mitchell gal ain't been wed more'n twenty-six months? Add that up.'

'Shut your ugly mouth,' Modesty snapped, her eyes blazing. 'You say another word an' Josh will kill you.'

'Why?' Houck had a look of mock surprise. 'Did he figure you were his virgin bride?'

'All the dogs in the street shall eat Jezebel,' Isaac warned.

The men went silent as they heard Josh stomping back in along the passage.

Modesty bit her lip, wondering if he had heard, and pretended to busy herself at the stove. She tensed herself for the inevitable whack across her buttocks.

'How's my li'l cattle queen?' Josh grabbed her hard into him and gave her a sloppy kiss. She instinctively turned her head and it landed on her cheek. He laughed, raucously.

'Why y'all gone quiet?' he asked, as he scrambled into his top-of-the-table chair. 'Come on, boys. Dig in.'

His brothers looked at Modesty and each other and snorted with laughter.

It was odd how, as soon as they were wed, Josh had turned from being an attentive, quavering courtier into a coarse, bullying husband. His word was law. She had no say. And in the bedroom Josh went at her like a bull in a china shop, then snored lustily the rest of the night.

On top of that she had to deal with the less than respectful behaviour of the other brothers, who treated her like she was their property, their tongues hanging out. Sometimes she felt like a prisoner in enemy territory. There was no way she could go back home. Gideon's new wife had proved to be a spoilt, senseless creature while Martha was reduced to the role of skivvy.

Cattle queen! she thought. Some empire to be trapped in for the rest of her life. More like 5,000 acres of lonesomeness.

★ ★ ★

It was early morning when Cal Mitchell stepped out from The Grotto on to the sidewalk at Goldfield to get a breath of fresh air and see some daylight. What he saw was an Oriental youth with long black hair, torn jacket, baggy loincloth and bare legs ride into town on a sweated-up mustang. Children on their way to school ran alongside poking sticks and laughing at his curious appearance.

Cal looked far more debonair and confident than he did two years before, in a hand-tailored brown tweed jacket, blue shirt with a loose bow, and narrow-legged whipcord pants over blood-red boots. He gave the youth a sympathetic smile, flicked away his cheroot and went back into the smoky casino where a poker game was still going on.

Higo paid for the mustang to be watered and fed at Garcia's livery and wandered back up the street. He decided he needed to look more American so, in an outfitters, bought tough-denim miner's jeans, white shirt, black jacket and broad-brimmed hat. He retained his comfortable sandals.

In this transformation he met no

objection when he entered a restaurant and devoured a hearty meal. His mind was still numbed by all the deaths, particularly Tama's. It was as if a glass wall separated him from these people. They barely existed for him. More like shadows on a screen. He knew he needed to move on. But first he had to equip himself with a weapon.

Opposite Garcia's was a blacksmith's from which the sound of hammer on anvil rang out. In the yard, Higo noticed a pile of discarded steel strips. He picked up a couple and took them inside. 'You make into sword for me,' he told the big black man, Jed Cooper, a freed slave who was gleaming with sweat as he stood over his forge.

Higo guessed he had time to spare. Spence's mustang had been the only one kept at the railhead camp. If Big Jim Hagerty followed on foot it would take him a day and night or more to cover the forty miles to Goldfield.

So, all day Jed heated and hammered the two pieces of steel, one hard, one soft, into one, encouraged partly by Higo's proffered greenback dollars, but also out of interest. He lost count of how many times he layered them together at the insistence of the Japanese youth.

'I am in luck!' Higo exclaimed, 'for this task should be done at the time of the August moon.'

Finally, he went outside and found some clay to coat on the blade to ensure it would cool slowly. Then it was heated for the last time and quenched in water.

Higo knew sword-making had a thousand-year history. The right to wear one belonged in the past to the elite. 'Now it is mine!' he cried, brandishing it, practising the moves he had learnt from his samurai lord.

'It's sharp as a razor,' Jed exclaimed, as he held up a newspaper for Higo to slash through. 'A fine sword. What'n hell you gonna use it for?'

'Thank you. You good man.' Higo bowed and held up the blade. 'Sword has one purpose — to kill enemy.'

When he went back over to the livery it was already dusk and the doors were barred. Higo went round the back, but there was no sign of Garcia, who had gone off to a nearby cantina. But a feisty stallion was prancing around a corral. A saddle and bridle were hung over a rail and a lariat looped on a post. 'My household gods are smiling on me today,' Higo said.

The stallion reared, whinnied and kicked out, but Higo got the saddle and bridle on him and leaped aboard. 'Go, my friend,' he shouted, steering him out of the open gate and galloping away out of town in the moonlight heading towards the south.

★　★　★

$500 REWARD — DEAD OR ALIVE, the poster blared. *Japanese youth, named Higo, 17 years, 5ft. 7ins., lean, mean, ugly, armed and dangerous. Wanted for rape, murder, robbery and horse theft.*

When Bill Hagerty limped into Goldfield on sore feet, suffering from heat and thirst, he had a ready audience. 'I got a mutiny,' he shouted. 'Some li'l Jap bastard's gone mad dog.'

When he had dosed himself with whiskey he had the poster printed and started nailing copies up around town. 'Any of you men willing to go in pursuit?' he asked a bunch of miners who had gathered round. 'This slitty-eyed Jap murdered two fine white men, my foreman and guard, without provocation, after he had raped and killed a Jap girl.'

The miners didn't look keen and wandered off to The Crystal Saloon where an old prospector told them, 'I ain't so sure I believe that story. Me an' my mule come past that railroad camp three days ago an' some young Jap was cooped up in a li'l cage out in the sun. There was a helluva a shindig goin' on

190

in a tent. Sounded like fellas drunk an' a gal's scream. Weren't none of my business so I went on my way.'

Cal Mitchell was standing at the bar having a beer and breakfast. 'You mean the gal weren't raped by the Jap but by them railroad men?' he called out.

'I ain't sayin' no more, but somethang fishy was goin' on,' the old desert rat declared.

Cornish Andy, the miner, remarked, 'Sounds to me like that Jap had reason to go mad dog.'

Cal had just finished his twelve-hour shift at the casino. Later in the morning he strolled down to the corral to take Nero for his daily gallop. 'Where's my stallion gone?' he asked Garcia, who had just woken up with a massive hangover.

Garcia had no idea, so he went over to the blacksmith's. 'You seen anything of Nero, Jed? Anybody suspicious hanging around last night?'

'No, only that Jap boy.'

'Jap? Hot damn. He's stolen my horse.'

They traversed the 200 miles from Goldfield across the bleak flats to Caliente in good time. Cal's other horse, a short-necked, deep-shouldered skewbald, might not be as fast as Nero, but he was sturdy. Yes, his hunch paid off. An odd-looking Oriental on a big stallion had paused there for refreshment. Instead of following Meadow Valley Wash he had headed into the forbidding ravines of the Badlands. Maybe he thought it would deter pursuit.

This time Cal had come prepared. The mule on a lead rein carried two barrels of fresh water. And an old Paiute, Uncle Jack, as he was called, swept his hand forward, pointing to almost indiscernible spoor, showing the way.

'You reckon it's Nero?' he asked.

Uncle Jack, in his worn buckskins and high-bowled hat turned his craggy face to him. 'Big horse.'

'Waal, he ain't having him.'

He did not relish entering the Maze again, but the Paiutes had lived there for a thousand years and knew how to get through. Talk made the mouth go dry so they barely spoke most of the day until the falling sun began to flush golden the massive walls towering hundreds of feet high, carved like ornate cathedrals, with windows in the rock, slender columns, arches and minarets.

'You think we're getting close?'

The Paiute shrugged. 'All I know is, he's lost.'

★ ★ ★

What devil has lured me into these intertwining ravines? Higo wondered. He must have wandered for fifty miles in the past two days seeking a way out. Both he and the stallion were suffering badly from thirst. The only vegetation appeared to be juniper trees or Douglas firs that stretched for the sun and reached top branches high out of the shadows. The foliage of juniper and its berries were bitter, useless for forage. But, as the shadows lengthened, Higo saw a dead tree that had lost the battle. He climbed to it, got a fire going. With one slash of his sword he had beheaded a horned lizard, which he eagerly roasted and ate. He tethered the stallion close by but he had no food or water to give him.

'The Great Sculptor must have taken aeons creating this masterpiece.' In spite of his exhaustion he could not help but marvel at the massive ramparts of rock. He prayed for the spirits of Tama, Mr Negato, poor Nanuki crushed by the girder and the clownish Kentaro, wishing them well on their journey. Then, flitting through his mind came memories of his family and comrades, the industrious peasants of the province of Echizen, of the snow whirling through the camphor trees, across the sacred bosom of Lake Biwa, his homeland, a land he might never see again. 'Brief is the time of pleasure.' Higo murmured the Buddhist refrain before he fell into a deep sleep. 'It quickly turns to pain. Whatsoever is born must necessarily die.'

* * *

Uncle Jack sniffed woodsmoke on the air. 'He not far ahead.'

'Yeah?' Cal jacked a shell into the breech of the Winchester. 'Let's leave the horses here, go ahead on foot.' It was almost dark, the moon yet to rise from behind the crags. 'Here, you take the rifle.' Cal eased the Remington from its holster and cocked it. 'Just give me back-up.' They padded along the flat bed of a ravine until the ground started to rise and they saw the flicker of a fire, the silhouette of a horse. 'Nero,' Cal whispered. 'Let's hope he don't whinny.'

'We downwind,' the Indian muttered.

They crept forward and saw the outline of a sleeping man huddled by the fire for the nights at this altitude grew cold. On the ground beside him was some sort of weapon.

Higo suddenly awakened to find a man straddling his chest, the cold steel of a revolver barrel pressed into his nose. He tried to wriggle free and reach for his sword but a moccasined foot clamped down on his wrist and the sword was tossed away.

'You make another move,' Cal hissed, 'and you're one dead sonuvagun.'

Higo shrugged, defeated. 'Kill me if you have to.'

The Paiute pressed the rifle barrel to Higo's forehead as Cal snapped manacles on to his wrists. 'Ain't no use struggling. We've got you, boy. Jack, why don't you go bring up the hosses? Nero could do with a drink.'

★ ★ ★

They had bound the Jap's ankles and tied him to the dead tree with the lariat. They cooked up a damper of flour and water in the fire's ashes and chewed on strips of jerked beef.

As he leaned back against a rock, a

tin mug of coffee in his hand, Cal drawled, 'Tell me something, pal, that Jap girl, did you, you know' — he made a motion with his free fist — 'rape her? Then kill her?'

'No.' Higo fired up. 'That is lie. She my girl. Hagerty throw me in cage. I hear Tama's screams. He, Spence and Somers rape her. In the night she throw herself off cliff. She has too much hurt and shame. I could do nothing.'

'How come Spence and Somers got killed!'

'We fight. They shoot fat Kentaro and Mr Negato. I kill them both. I wish I had kill Hagerty, too.'

'But you ran, instead?'

'Yes, I run. Now, you got me. You take me back to hang.'

'There's five hundred dollars on your head.'

They sat in silence for a while watching the flames.

'Hell, I don't need the money,' Cal said. 'How about you, Jack? You wanna take him back?'

Jack shrugged. 'He ain't done nuthin' to me. I just come along as tracker. Figure you owe me fifty dollar for that.'

'I want go back. Kill Hagerty.'

'You can't do that. We need his darn railroad. Anyhow, you'd never get a fair trial.'

Cal grinned and peeled off sixty from a roll in his pocket and tossed them across. 'Thanks, Jack. Tomorrow you can both clear out. I know the way from here. I'm going on to Zion. Higo, take my skewbald. Head south.'

It was as if a strong magnetic urge was luring him on. Although he feared the worst.

The Indian peered at the weird shapes of the ravines. 'My people believe these hoodoo formations are evil people turned into rocks.'

'I wish it was as easy as that,' Cal muttered, ''cause there's a helluva lot of evil men where I'm going.'

11

He climbed Nero up a steep ascent to the high plateau, the mule jogging along behind, and, on down beneath the great thousand-foot-high cliff, past the burned-out cabin where he had been born, down into the Virgin River ravine which was mostly in shadow enclosed by vertical walls on either side.

There was always a serenity down there, the silence broken only by the placid flow of the river, the croaking of tree frogs as he waded the animals through the deeper parts. A bunch of long-eared mule deer, grazing beneath a willow, gazed at him then raced for safety. But it was not animals he was hunting.

Then he was out in the rugged valley with mountains rising 4,000 feet into the sky, which Mormon settlers had named Court of the Patriarchs, Angel's

Landing, and so forth. He recalled Gideon saying, 'We Mitchells have no need for a temple. This valley is our temple.'

He by-passed his former home and rode across the grassland, straight as an arrow, towards Temperance.

The few folk about on the dusty main street, women in sunbonnets, muffled in long dresses, their work-worn men, regarded him as if he were a ghost. Could this well-turned out stranger be that wild Mitchell boy they had known?

It was as if it were foreordained. There outside the general store was Martha, holding the reins of a wagon, as if about to leave. And Modesty! His heart gave a leap. Could it be possible? She had a baby, swaddled in a shawl, in her arms.

'Cal!' She, too, stared at him as if he were a ghost. 'What are you doing here?'

'I've come for you, Modesty.' He rode up to her. 'I want you to come away with me. I'm a wealthy man these days. I own a casino in Goldfield.'

'A gambling house? Satan's hellhole? Well, that suits you,' Martha exclaimed. 'Huccome you own it?'

'My friend, Mr McLintock, died two months ago and left it to me, lock, stock and barrel. I'm offering you a good life, Modesty.'

'Huh!' Martha shrieked. 'You think you can just ride in here — '

'Cal!' Modesty showed him the baby. 'I'm married to Josh Granger.'

'Josh?' he cried. 'You sure didn't waste much time. And that's his?'

'Cal, what did you expect me to do?' Her dark, lustrous eyes burned into him, pleading. Then she took a deep breath and blurted out, 'This is Daniel. He's ours. I mean yours. But we belong to Josh now.'

'Mine?' This was one piece of information he hadn't expected. 'Josh? How do you mean?'

'Don't tell the whole town,' Martha hissed. 'You two, come with me. I got somethang to tell you.'

She led the way into the Vienna restaurant, sang out for coffees and sat them down at a table. 'Guess it's somethang I shoulda told ya a long time ago.' Martha was aware that things were not right between Josh and her daughter and had made her own big decision. 'You two ain't brother and sister.'

'What?' Cal was dumbfounded. After all these years it was as if a great weight had been lifted from his shoulders. 'What do you mean?'

Martha waited, discreetly, until the waitress had served them. 'Modesty is my daughter. But you, Cal, are the son of a woman I knew. No relative. When she and her man were killed, their cabin burned down, I stole you and raised you as my own.'

'Mother,' Modesty pleaded, 'why didn't you tell us before? This changes everything.'

'So,' Cal demanded. 'Who was my mother?'

'All I know is she was called Greten,

a good young woman, even if she left her husband, Isaac Granger and ran off with another man. He built that cabin up on the hill. He was a Swede; that's where you get your blond thatch from.'

'Yes,' he said, wonderingly. 'The burned-out cabin. It's as if I knew this all along. What else do you know about *him*?'

'He was a fine, hard-working man. Even if they were sinners there was no reason for them to be killed. It was wrong.'

Jacob Granger's wife peered through a curtain across the doorway to the kitchen, watching and listening. 'Lucy,' she hissed, 'go tell the boy to ride fast to the ranch. Tell the boys Cal Mitchell's here. And he's got Josh's wife.'

★ ★ ★

'It's no good, Cal,' Modesty cried, as he helped her back up on to the wagon. 'I can't do it. Josh adores Daniel. I can't

203

take him from him.' She shook her head, her eyes troubled. 'Anyway, they wouldn't let me. It's best you go.'

Cal put out a finger to the infant who gurgled, clutching hold of it. 'See, he's mine. He should be with us, not the lousy Grangers.'

Martha was gathering the reins. 'Leave them alone, Cal. It's too late. Go back to where you came from.'

'No,' he insisted, but froze in his tracks as a gruff voice rang out and he turned to see James Houck standing on the sidewalk across the street.

'Mitchell, you quit pestering that gal,' Houck shouted. 'I knew you'd come back. I been waiting for you.'

Houck was swinging a heavy Volcanic, .50–.95 calibre, specially converted, with a twelve-inch barrel and a claw grip, holding it down by his right thigh. A mocking grin spread across his dark features. 'You've asked for it this time.'

'Is that the cannon you blasted a hole in my brother Jedediah with?' Cal replied, stepping away from the wagon towards the centre of the street so nobody else would get hurt.

'Maybe it is.' Houck jumped down to face him. 'You wanna find out what it does to your insides?'

'I know what it does,' Cal said, unbuttoning his jacket and pulling it aside to reveal the Remington .44 holstered across his loins. 'Maybe you'd prefer a taste of this?'

Houck shrugged, sure of himself. 'Any time you're ready.'

'How about now?' Cal brought the Remington out and fired as he stepped to one side. He fanned the filed-down hammer and kept on firing, gritting his teeth as Houck's cannon boomed and flashed fire and smoke.

Houck staggered, levered one last shot, and collapsed into the dust, his murky eyes bulging beneath his curly mop. Blood began to ooze through his black shirt from his chest. 'So,' he gasped, 'ye've been improvin' your aim.'

'Maybe.' Cal looked around in case

the sheriff had support, but could see no danger.

Houck's left hand slid to the short-barrelled .32 holstered on his hip. He snarled like a wounded animal as he raised it —

'Cal!' Modesty screamed. 'Look out!'

Cal spun round and unerringly put his sixth bullet into Houck's heart before he could fire.

He went over and poked him with his foot to make sure he was dead.

He heard Martha shout and turned to see her whipping the wagon horses away.

'Cal,' Modesty screamed from her seat on the wagon as they passed. 'Please! Go!'

He watched the wagon go careering out of town. He collected Nero and, with the mule in tow, rode back the way he had come.

12

He had come through the river's ravine to reach the high ground. He knew they would come after him but, on an impulse, he nosed Nero through the Slit, lashing his quirt to urge him and the mule up the steep incline. When he reached the arch he jumped down and hauled them through, up to the cave. Here he would make his stand. For an hour or so he hid on the rim, looking down, listening for sounds of pursuit. Suddenly he saw a rider coming, kicking up dust, and he squinted along the Winchester's sights, taking aim. No! It was *her*.

'What you doin' here?' he called, as she dragged her mustang up to join him.

'I had to come,' Modesty cried, the wind flattening her dress against the curves of her slim body. 'Cal, this time they really intend to kill you. You must go on.'

'Hmm!' He made a scoffing, guttural sound. 'I ain't runnin' no more. I'm stopping here. If they come, they come. That's an end of it. You're a married woman. You head back where you come from. Fast, before they find you here.'

His grey eyes in his narrow, handsome face were as hard as flints and alert as he stood there, rifle in hand. 'Go on, git. I don't want you.'

'You know you do.' She pressed the rifle aside and slid into his arms. 'I'm leaving him, Cal. I don't want his name no more. We can get away if we go now.'

His face had a haunted look, his thick flaxen hair hanging back over the knot of his bandanna. 'It's too late. You know that.'

Suddenly it was like two years before, unable to resist, clamped in each other's arms, nibbling at each other's face and hair. He put a protective arm around her, led her back into the cave, laid her down on his bedroll and dipped his head to kiss her sweet, gentle face, her upraised succulent lips as she wound her arms and thighs around him.

'What if ol' Gideon could see us now,' he said, afterwards. 'Fornicators!'

'I don't like that word, Cal. It's ugly.'

'Yeah, all that sermonizing didn't do me much good. Look at me now, a gambler, a fast gun, a killer.'

'At least you're not my brother.' She stroked fingers down his ribcage. 'I no longer feel guilty about this.'

The mule's raucous braying alerted him. 'We got visitors. An' that damn mule's showing 'em the way.'

His heart was pounding as he ducked out of the cave and peered over the rim. 'The whole clan,' he muttered, 'Noah, Jacob, Paul, Ephraim. Your husband's down there, too, and Uncle Isaac.'

'It's that uncle of theirn who's poisoned their minds.' Modesty buttoned her dress as she knelt beside him. 'Josh never really wanted this. Leave him out of it, Cal.'

'He's here, isn't he?'

She was surprised by the bitterness of his tone. 'I'm frightened, Cal.'

'I'm sceered of dyin', too, Modesty, but I gotta face up to it.' He had never understood Isaac Granger's burning hatred, his undying grudge against him. Until now.

He raised himself and shouted down to the men a hundred yards below. 'Come on! What you waiting for? I'm warning you, I'm shooting to kill.'

They scrambled from their horses, shouting and pointing upwards. Ephraim raised his single-shot Sharps he had used in the war. The bullet took off Cal's earlobe as it hissed past his head.

'Christ!' he yelped, but trained his rifle on Ephraim's chest as he began to reload. He took first pressure on the trigger. And squeezed. Ephraim was bowled backwards, the bullet through his heart. 'Got him!'

The Grangers let loose a fusillade of lead. The attack scorched chips from the rocks about them. Cal was hard-pressed to make accurate reply. He could only raise himself to take quick pots with the Winchester as the Grangers dodged from rock to rock, working their way upwards.

The oily lawyer, Isaac, was at the rear, urging his troops on. Cal had him in his sights. But his bullet whined harmlessly past as Isaac slipped and fell flat. Cal levered his Winchester again and hit Paul in his boot, making him hop.

The fourteen in his rifle's magazine were gone. 'Here!' He handed it to Modesty and pushed a box of a dozen cartridges across. 'Reload.'

Cal pulled out his Remington and crashed out slugs at the Grangers as they climbed close, without success. 'Hot damn, I jest cain't win.'

'You sure cain't.'

Cal froze. Jacob had somehow climbed up around and was perched on a rock behind them.

'Don't make a move,' Jacob snarled. 'Or I'll shatter your spine. Toss that gun away. Raise your hands.'

Why not? Cal spun around to make a

snap shot. But there was an ominous click. The Remington, too, was empty.

The weasel-faced Jacob hooted with laughter, then saw Modesty with the Winchester ready to fire. 'Go on, sister-in-law. I dare you.'

'Don't,' Cal said, pressing the rifle aside and tossing down the Remington. 'Leave her out of this. It's me you want. Do what you have to do.'

Isaac Granger clambered up to join them. 'Rope 'em, boys.'

'What, her, too?' Noah asked.

'Both of them, I said.'

'What say you, Josh?' Jacob roped Cal's wrists tight and placed a noose around his throat, jerking it tight. 'You gonna hang your own wife? What about your kid?'

For reply, Joshua stepped forward and backhanded Modesty hard across the jaw with a leather-gloved fist, knocking her to her knees. 'I come to the conclusion he ain't my kid. He's theirn.'

'Josh!' Blood trickled from Modesty's

lip as she pleaded. 'You can't do this. It's brutal murder. It's you they'll hang.'

Joshua brushed her imploring hands away, contemptuously. 'You tricked me into marrying you.' He hawked and spat in her face. 'Take the whore.'

'Where?' Noah asked, as he noosed her, too, dragged her to her feet and forced her to climb on her mustang. 'There ain't no hangin' trees round here for miles.'

'How about the arch?' The thin-faced Jacob pointed down the slope to the high, natural curved formation of rock. 'We can sling ropes over that.'

Cal suddenly tried to burst away, kicking out, but they held on to him. 'Not her,' he shouted. 'It ain't right. I'm the one to blame.'

But the Granger brothers' faces were grimly merciless as they heaved him on to his stallion. In silence they led their two prisoners down the slope, stationed them under the arch and snaked the ropes over it, fixing the nooses tight to spurs of rock.

'Hang 'em,' Jacob yelled. 'Are we all agreed?'

Young Paul had limped up to them, blood seeping from his boot, using his rifle as a crutch. 'I am,' he said, and the others nodded in one accord.

'You ain't so flash clever now, are you Mitchell?' Noah sneered. 'What you come back for, anyhow? Just to cause trouble?'

'I was raised here. You ain't got God-given rights to these parts.'

'Yes,' Isaac agreed, 'but you always were a viper in our midst. And now you've proved you ain't changed. Have you anything else to say before we execute you?'

'You're a lawyer,' Modesty blurted out. 'How can you do this?'

'In the town I practise people's law. Up here we go by God's law. The Bible says 'If a man shall take his sister it is a wicked thing and both shall be cut off'.'

'So happens she ain't my sister, and you know that,' Cal growled. 'Your wife left you for another man, Sven

Lundgren, no doubt because she couldn't stand you, you heinous bastard. You never got over it, did you?'

'Don't listen to him, boys, he's lying.'

'He knows this is the truth. Him and your father and other men went up there, burned the cabin, killed them both. They were my mother and father.'

'Is that right, Isaac?' Josh asked.

'Of course it's right. Martha's just told us. She went up there, rescued me, and raised me as a Mitchell. That's why he's always hated me. He knows it's the truth.'

Isaac Granger brandished his Bible, screaming at them. 'So what if it is the truth? The Lord says 'He that commits adultery with another man's wife both the adulterer and the adulteress shall surely be put to death'. Leviticus. These two must both be hanged.'

'Get on with it then,' Cal growled, 'you mealy-mouthed hypocrite.'

Isaac Granger's thin lips smiled bitterly as if his lifetime's ambition had been achieved. He slapped at the haunches of the stallion with his Bible. It sprang forward leaving Cal dangling, kicking, choking in space as Modesty screamed, 'No!'

Suddenly, Higo rode in among them, slashing his sword about him like a whirlwind. He severed the rope and Cal hit the dust hard. He cut back into the startled Josh's jugular as he fumbled with his six-gun and blood spouted. He spun the skewbald and cut Modesty free. Noah raised his Sharps, but his shot went wild as Higo hacked off his arm. The stallion reared and kicked out at Jacob, adding to the confusion. Cal was on his feet, holding out his wrists and Higo's razor-sharp blade released him. Cal grabbed Josh's revolver and, as Paul tried to retaliate, sent him tumbling with a bullet through his throat. Jacob now had his rifle trained on him. Cal hurled it aside and put a bullet point blank into his heart.

The lawyer was backing away out of the bedlam of smoke and dust, holding up his Bible as if it would protect him from this strange vicious Oriental who had appeared, it seemed, out of nowhere. Terror in him, he turned and ran.

Higo galloped his horse after him. A sensation of glory filled his soul as if he were propelled by the Divine Wind — the *kamikaze* — that blew away the Mongol hordes' invasion fleet at Akarta Bay in the thirteenth century. He swung the samurai sword with careful force and precision and lopped off Isaac Granger's head. It went rolling down the slope trailing blood and came to a halt, eyes bulging, mouth agape as if trying to speak.

Higo leapt from his horse and strode back amid the corpses. He was bare-chested, his muscled body rippling like whipcord as he held the sword aloft and plunged it into the writhing Noah to silence him.

Then he bowed to Cal. 'My debt to you is repaid.'

Cal looked about him with astonishment, holding his throat and rasped

217

out, huskily, 'Yes, I guess it is.'

Higo released Modesty's bonds. 'Evil men,' he said. 'They deserved to die.'

★   ★   ★

Martha emerged from the Canyon of Spirits as they rode away from the cave. 'Wait for us,' she called, as she came splashing through on the back of a mustang, baby Daniel in a papoose board on her back. 'We're coming with you.'

Cal dabbed his bandanna at his bloody ear lobe and grinned widely at Modesty. 'You didn't tell me the ma-in-law was included in the package.'

'Gideon's welcome to his fancy bit,' Martha said. 'I'm cuttin' loose. Where are the Grangers?'

'We cleaned out the whole nest of rats,' Cal replied. 'The whole damn lot thanks to Higo who arrived in the nick of time. It was a bloodbath.'

'I sensed you had trouble. I hung around. When I heard shooting I come fast.' Higo glanced up at the sky. 'The buzzards will soon clean up their bones.'

They put spurs to their horses and headed away from Zion, past the burned-out cabin and its ghosts, riding up on to the high plateau.

'Head for the border.' Cal pointed south then shook Higo's hand in farewell. 'You only got Apaches to worry about in Arizona. They might even adopt you into their tribe! Or head on to Mexico. There's some nice l'il *señoritas* down there, so I've heard!'

They watched him go, then, as the sun began its descent, rode down into the roseate cauldron of the Badlands and on to Goldfield.

'One day,' Cal muttered, 'I'll avenge Higo. I'll force that man Hagerty into a fight.'

We do hope that you have enjoyed reading this large print book.

Did you know that all of our titles are available for purchase?

We publish a wide range of high quality large print books including:
Romances, Mysteries, Classics
General Fiction
Non Fiction and Westerns

Special interest titles available in large print are:
The Little Oxford Dictionary
Music Book, Song Book
Hymn Book, Service Book

Also available from us courtesy of Oxford University Press:
Young Readers' Dictionary
(large print edition)
Young Readers' Thesaurus
(large print edition)

For further information or a free brochure, please contact us at:
Ulverscroft Large Print Books Ltd.,
The Green, Bradgate Road, Anstey,
Leicester, LE7 7FU, England.
Tel: (00 44) **0116 236 4325**
Fax: (00 44) **0116 234 0205**

HIDEOUT AT
MENDER'S CROSSING

John Glasby

The ghost town of Mender's Crossing is the ideal base for a gang of outlaws operating without interference. When a group of soldiers is killed defending a gold-train, the army calls upon special operator Steve Landers to investigate. However, Landers is also up against land baron Hal Clegg: his hired mercenaries are driving independent ranchers from their land. He will need nerves of steel to succeed when he is so heavily outnumbered. Can he cheat the odds and win?

DEAD MAN RIDING

Lance Howard

Two years ago Logan Priest left the woman he loved to shelter her from the dangers of his profession . . . but he made a terrible mistake. A vicious outlaw whom he brought to justice escapes prison and seeks revenge on the very woman that Priest had sought to protect. Logan is forced to return to the manhunting trail when he receives the outlaw's grisly calling card. Can he meet the challenge, or will he become the killer's next victim?

TO DIE THIS DAY

Clint Ryker

The rich and powerful Traffords are relieved when their eldest son, Tom, returns home safely to the family ranch after the war. When his wartime partner and hero, Clayton Grady, shows up too, the homecoming celebrations rock the county. How could veteran Grady know that this seemingly happy event would, in time, tear his family apart and lead to a nightmare of deceit, suspicion and bloody murder, as horrific as anything he had encountered during the war . . .

HANGTREE COUNTY

Hank J. Kirby

Drew Hardy always found himself overshadowed by his brothers, Kerry and Luke. Then he was jailed for attempted murder. Four years later, a twist of fate sets him free. But would freedom mean working for Kerry and Luke whilst they ensured he never got his share of the family ranch? He must settle the matter with guns — time in jail had taught him plenty about those. Now, for the first time, Drew was a force to be reckoned with.